He lay on his back, his dead eyes staring up at nothing. He wore a T-shirt identical to his brother's, except that the arrow pointed to the right.

And except for the blood, quite a bit of it, almost obscuring the arrow and the wording.

Rhodes always felt a hollow sadness when he saw a dead body. Maybe it was pity. There was something about the absence of light in the eyes that affected him. Terry Crawford might not have been of much account, but he didn't deserve to be killed for no reason and left to lie in a dry field for the buzzards to find. Or the sheriff.

No buzzards yet, but they'd be along soon enough if he didn't get the body moved. That couldn't be done until the crime scene had been worked.

★

Bill Crider

OF ALL SAD WORDS

W🌐RLDWIDE.

TORONTO • NEW YORK • LONDON
AMSTERDAM • PARIS • SYDNEY • HAMBURG
STOCKHOLM • ATHENS • TOKYO • MILAN
MADRID • WARSAW • BUDAPEST • AUCKLAND

Recycling programs
for this product may
not exist in your area.

OF ALL SAD WORDS

A Worldwide Mystery/March 2009

First published by St. Martin's Press, LLC.

ISBN-13: 978-0-373-26665-4
ISBN-10:   0-373-26665-0

Printed in U.S.A.

To all the gang at Dooley's Pub

ONE

WHEN HE WAS in high school, Sheriff Dan Rhodes had been compelled to memorize poetry. Unfortunately, very little of it had stuck with him over the years since. He had a vague recollection of a mountaineer whose fist was a knotty hammer, and he recalled that lives of great men all remind us of something or other, but that was about it. In fact, the only rhyming lines he remembered were a couple that went "of all sad words of tongue or pen / The saddest are these: 'It might have been!'"

Rhodes, having had those words stuck in his head for a large part of his life, might even have believed them at one time. Now, however, he was convinced that they were baloney. The saddest words of all were "It seemed like a good idea at the time."

Not that the Citizens' Sheriff's Academy hadn't been a good idea in some ways. It created a lot of interest, it had informed people about the sheriff's department and county government, and it had generated some nice publicity for the department.

But things had gotten out of hand.

"You've created a bunch of vigilantes is what you've done," Jack Parry told Rhodes.

Parry was the county judge. He had a fringe of white hair around his head and a round pink face that was always shaved close. If he'd had a beard, a red suit, and some granny glasses, he'd have looked like Santa Claus. Sometimes he was almost as cheerful as old Santa, but this wasn't one of those times.

He didn't dress like Santa, either. He wore a navy blue suit, a white shirt, and a blue-and-red-striped tie. He had on some kind of fancy shaving lotion that Rhodes, being an Aqua Velva man, couldn't identify.

"I think you're wrong," Rhodes told him. "We don't have any vigilantes."

"I'm the county judge. I'm never wrong. Well, hardly ever. I made the mistake of speaking to that academy of yours. I should have stayed home and watched the Astros game."

"They lost," Rhodes said.

"That was three weeks ago. How can you remember?"

"They lose a lot."

Parry shook his head. "I know it. I don't even know why I watch them. But even if they'd lost by ten runs, it would have been better than standing in front of those wild-eyed radicals you brought together."

Rhodes and Parry were sitting in Parry's chambers, located in a big corner room of the county courthouse. Rhodes also had an office in the courthouse, but his was sparsely furnished and seldom used. If the cleaning staff hadn't visited it regularly, it would have had cobwebs hanging from the light fixture.

Parry, however, had an oak desk with a leather top, floor-to-ceiling bookshelves filled with what Rhodes assumed were law books and commentaries, comfortable leather chairs for his visitors, and even a little refrigerator. Rhodes had never seen what was kept in the refrigerator. He sometimes wondered if there might be a Dr Pepper or two.

"You think Randy Lawless is a wild-eyed radical?" Rhodes said.

Lawless was a lawyer, probably the most prosperous one in Blacklin County. He looked more like a Republican legislator, which he had been for a couple of terms, than any wild-eyed radical Rhodes could imagine, which is why he'd offered Lawless as an example.

"Not him," Parry said. He paused and leaned back in his chair. "He's too busy making money on his court cases to cause any trouble for the county, unless maybe it's for you when he defends somebody you've arrested. Come to think of it, though, he does drive an Infiniti. That's pretty radical for around here."

Rhodes could think of at least one case in the not too distant past in which Lawless had defended a client against a murder charge, but that was his job. Rhodes didn't hold it against him.

"What about Max Schwartz?" Rhodes said.

"You're getting warmer."

Schwartz was one of two newcomers to the county who'd attended the academy. He'd arrived in Clearview about ten months earlier, behind the wheel of a red Chrysler convertible, with his blond wife at his side and a big dog, a black Lab, in the backseat.

Schwartz claimed that he'd left his law practice in Kentucky because of burnout and that he'd started driving, until he'd found a small town that appealed to him and had a business opportunity that he couldn't pass up. Why he thought Clearview needed a music store was anybody's guess, but he'd rented a building in the downtown area, such as it was, and opened up to as much fanfare as the chamber of commerce could provide. If you wanted to buy a guitar or a clarinet, Schwartz was your man. He'd already joined the Lions Club, and his wife worked with the town's newly created amateur theatrical group, the Clearview Players.

"His convertible's red," Rhodes said. "He could be a Communist."

"Now you're just messing with me," Parry said. "Anyway, there aren't any more Communists since the Berlin Wall got knocked down. You know who I'm talking about."

Rhodes knew all right. Parry's wild-eyed radical was the other newcomer, Dr. C. P. Benton. Benton was chairman of the math department at the community college branch that had opened in temporary quarters in downtown Clearview several years ago. The enrollment had grown so much that there was now an actual campus on one of the highways outside of town. Many of the instructors had homes in or around Clearview now, instead of commuting into town for their classes, and Benton was one of them.

Though he was a member of the community, he didn't look like anybody else in town. What hair he had was often in wild disarray, he'd been seen carrying a guitar case, and he referred to his rented house as the "Casa de Math." He didn't mow his lawn much, either. He even had a beard—neatly trimmed, but still a beard. Clearly, he wasn't a man to be trusted.

"He claims he moved here because of a broken heart," Rhodes said.

Parry nodded. "He's mooning after some woman down in a little town called Hughes, around Houston. Sally something or other. They taught at the community college down there."

"You know more about him than I do," Rhodes said, but he knew a few other things. So did Parry, and Rhodes figured he'd get around to mentioning them.

Sure enough, Parry said, "He's been coming to the commissioner's court meetings."

The commissioner's court had nothing to do with the dispensing of justice, even though it was presided over by the county judge. It was the county's governing body, and each of the county's precincts elected a commissioner to sit on it. Among other things, it set the tax rates and saw to the building and maintenance of county roads and bridges, as well as all other county facilities, including the jail. The court's meetings were open to the public, but Parry wasn't happy when too many questions got asked. He and the commissioners were used to having things pretty much their own way.

"Dr. Benton's just interested in being a part of the community," Rhodes said. "That's why he wanted to be in the academy."

"He's nosy," Parry said, dismissing all other motives. "And he's a complainer. Won't mow his lawn, but he's worried about the ditches."

Benton lived on a county road a couple of miles from the college. Rhodes knew he'd complained a couple of times about the maintenance of the ditches along the road, requesting that they be mowed more regularly.

"You won't have to worry about his lawn, and he won't have to worry about the ditches if it doesn't rain soon," Rhodes said. "The lawn and the weeds will all be dead."

"He's starting to ask about appraisal caps," Parry said. "He's a troublemaker."

Anybody who both complained about road maintenance and asked about appraisal caps was a troublemaker in Parry's book, even if citizens were more or less expected to do those things.

"Mikey Burns agrees with me," Parry added.

Burns, whose name was Michael, was the commissioner in Benton's district. According to county legend, Burns had been labeled "Mikey" by his older brother because he'd eat anything, like some kid in an old TV commercial. His brother claimed Mikey would eat worms and dirt and said that he'd once eaten part of an old bicycle tire. Rhodes was willing to believe the first two, but he wasn't so sure about the tire.

"I called down to Hughes," Parry continued. "Talked to some cop down there." He looked out the window, thinking. "Weems. That's the cop's name. He says Benton got involved in a couple of murders down there."

Rhodes had heard about that, too. Benton had told the academy class about it one evening.

"If by 'involved' you mean he chased down a killer, you're right."

Parry snorted. He's pretty good at it, Rhodes thought.

"He was just in the right place at the right time. That Sally woman did most of the solving, and she nearly got herself killed. Benton was more of a hindrance than anything else. Damned vigilantes, both of them."

Rhodes shrugged. None of what Parry had to say bothered him. Of course, Parry hadn't even gotten around to the outside agitators yet.

"I think Benton's all right," Rhodes said. "A little weird, maybe, but he's not going to destroy the county government. He might even be a radical, but he's not wild-eyed."

Parry leaned forward, resting his elbows on the leather desktop, and looked at Rhodes.

"You just wait," Parry said. "When he starts trying to do your job for you, you'll change your tune. I know he's been complaining to you, too."

Down the road from Benton's house, around a curve and back off in some woods, there was a mobile home that Benton suspected of being a meth lab. He'd called the sheriff's department a couple of times and asked that someone investigate.

Rhodes thought Benton could be right. The two men who lived in the mobile home were twin brothers, Larry and Terry Crawford. They both had records, though they'd never been known to traffic in drugs. And while meth dealers were usually consumers of their own product, the Crawfords didn't show any of the usual signs of deterioration that users did.

Ruth Grady, one of the deputies, got the assignment of checking out the Crawfords' activities, but she hadn't been able to do much so far. To get to the mobile home, she would have had to go through a gate that was chained shut. Without any evidence other than Benton's complaints, there was no way she could have gotten a search warrant, so she'd stopped at the gate.

"Dr. Benton doesn't want to do my job for me," Rhodes told Parry. "He might want a thing or two investigated, and that's why the academy was good for him. We explain to people the way the county government works, we give them a short course in how the law's enforced, and we take them on a tour of the jail. We don't teach them to be vigilantes."

"You didn't mention the ride-along," Parry said.

People who signed up for the academy were allowed to ride with one of the deputies for a shift or two if they requested it. Benton had asked for a ride with Ruth Grady. Rhodes thought maybe Benton liked her.

"The ride-along's part of learning about enforcement," Rhodes said.

"Then there's the crime-scene investigation. You forget about that?"

"Enforcement," Rhodes said. "Everybody loves crime-scene investigation."

"Just like on TV," Parry said, and they both had a laugh. Blacklin County wasn't quite in the same league with the TV cops on the various CSI shows.

"What about the shooting range?" Parry said.

For years, the county officers had driven elsewhere to qualify on the shooting range, and some of the academy members had been invited to see what it was like.

"Hardly anybody actually fired a sidearm," Rhodes said.

"Lawless did. Schwartz did."

Parry has spies everywhere, Rhodes thought.

"Lawyers with guns," Parry said, shaking his head. "Not a good combination."

An old song lyric popped into Rhodes's head: "Send lawyers, guns and money."

"They didn't shoot anybody," he said. "They were pretty good on the range, though."

"Probably have concealed-carry permits," Parry said. "Next time there's a stickup, they'll do your job for you."

Rhodes hadn't heard anybody say stickup in a long time.

"You'll see," Parry went on. "This isn't going to turn out well."

Rhodes thought he was wrong, but he didn't want to argue anymore. He'd been called in, he'd appeared, and Parry had had his say. Rhodes had answered as best he could, and now he was ready to leave, unless Parry had a joke for him. The judge was fond of jokes when he was in a better mood.

If he had a joke this time, he didn't have time to tell it. The telephone on his desk rang. It was an old-fashioned black one, the kind you hardly ever saw. Rhodes wondered why Parry didn't have a newer model. Maybe he thought he was saving money for the county.

"I told Louise not to interrupt us," Parry said, but he picked up the phone and answered it. He listened for a second and handed the phone to Rhodes. "It's for you."

Rhodes took the phone and said hello.

"Sheriff?"

It was Hack Jensen, the dispatcher.

"It's me, Hack. Go ahead."

"You better get out to County Road Four eighty-six where it crosses the creek," Hack said. "There's been an accident."

"What happened?"

"Trailer house blew up," Hack said.

C. P. Benton lived on County Road 486. The mobile home he'd complained about was near the creek.

"The Crawford brothers," Rhodes said.

"Yep."

Rhodes told Hack he'd get started, then handed the phone back to Parry.

"Trouble?" Parry said, hanging up the phone.

He drove away and was soon followed by the ambulance, Ruth Grady, Benton, and the fire trucks. Only Jennifer Loam, the fire chief, and Rhodes remained.

A man named Parker was the fire chief. He and Rhodes had worked together on a case or two before, most recently one involving a dead man whose body had been found in a burning house. Jennifer had been right there for that one, too.

Rhodes thought that Parker looked relieved that this time there wasn't a body, though it was hard to see his face under the helmet he wore. Parker took off the helmet and wiped his face with his hand.

"What do you think happened to Terry Crawford?" he asked.

Rhodes shook his head. "I don't have any idea. What do you think caused the explosion?"

Parker looked at Jennifer and her little recording device. "Hard to be sure at this point."

"You can make a guess, can't you?" Rhodes said.

Parker shook his head. "I don't like to guess."

"I won't hold you to it, and neither will Ms. Loam. This is off the record."

Jennifer gave Rhodes a look, but she nodded and turned off the recorder.

"Could the Crawfords have been running a meth lab out of this place?" Rhodes said when he was sure Jennifer was no longer recording.

"Well," Parker said, "that's a possibility, but I don't think it's what caused the explosion."

Rhodes was surprised, but then he realized he should have known it couldn't have been a meth explosion, not if there wasn't a lab.

He was almost certain there hadn't been a meth lab. He'd have smelled it if there had been any trace. For that matter, people living nearby, even someone as far away as Benton, would have smelled it long ago. No matter what Benton thought he'd seen, he hadn't smelled anything, not that he'd mentioned to Rhodes at any rate.

"What do you think was the problem?" he asked.

"I think the propane tank blew up," Parker told him.

Rhodes thought, but broken and flattened weeds showed that someone had passed that way not too long before, headed in the direction of the creek.

Rhodes followed the fresh trail down toward the trees that lined the creek. From the side of the hill, he could see that only a thin stream of water, hardly more than an inch deep and less than a foot wide, trickled through the creek bed. Rhodes remembered a time not so long ago when the water had run deep and swift enough to expose the bones of a mammoth. A lot more was exposed before that episode was over, he thought, hoping that he wouldn't make any grim discoveries.

But he did. He was almost to the creek when he found Terry Crawford. He lay on his back, his dead eyes staring up at nothing. He wore a T-shirt identical to his brother's, except that the arrow pointed to the right.

And except for the blood, quite a bit of it, almost obscuring the arrow and the wording.

Rhodes always felt a hollow sadness when he saw a dead body. Maybe it was pity. There was something about the absence of light in the eyes that affected him. Terry Crawford might not have been of much account, but he didn't deserve to be killed for no reason and left to lie in a dry field for the buzzards to find. Or the sheriff.

Rhodes looked away, first down to the dry creek bed and then up at the cloudless sky. No buzzards yet, but they'd be along soon enough if he didn't get the body moved. That couldn't be done until the crime scene had been worked.

A grasshopper hummed past. Rhodes swatted at it and missed. Then he started back up the hill.

"WELL, IT'S OBVIOUS that he didn't die in the explosion," Ruth Grady said.

Rhodes nodded. He'd called Ruth on the radio and told her to come back because he wanted her to work the scene.

"The JP should be here in a few minutes," Rhodes said. "The ambulance is on the way back, too. You see what you can find out here, and I'll go tell Larry about his brother."

"He's not going to take it well."

"You think?" Rhodes said.

RHODES COULD HAVE driven to Obert on the county road, but he went back to the highway and took that route. He'd worked a few cases in Obert, the most recent one involving the rock crusher that had moved into town, blasting away at the limestone hill where Obert sat, the highest point in the county. As a result of a murder and a conviction, the rock crusher had been shut down. It would eventually be sold, and the blasting would start again, but that would take quite some time. Meanwhile, the residents of Obert had a little break from the noise, dust, and disruptions.

Obert, as even its residents would have had to admit, wasn't much of a town. Its population was around four hundred, and only a few buildings and stores remained. Most of them faced the highway that was the town's main street. One of the buildings was Jamey Hamilton's barbershop. Rhodes parked in front of it and got out of the car.

A short red-and-white barber pole hung on the brick wall, and a sign that said closed hung on the inside of the glass door. Rhodes rattled the doorknob and tapped on the glass, but nobody showed up. He peered through the glass and saw only a barber chair and a couple of regular chairs for the customers.

Rhodes went next door to Michal Schafer's Antiques Emporium. A black-and-white cat slept, unmoving, in a window display that included a couple of old school lunch boxes with Disney cartoon characters on them, a few dishes with designs that might have been hand-painted, a couple of motors for ceiling fans, a board with samples of different kinds of barbed wire attached to it, and three lightning rod arrows with colored glass where there would have been feathers on an actual arrow.

Rhodes opened the door and went inside, causing an overhead bell to jingle. Michal was in the back of the large, dimly lit room, standing behind an old candy counter that held baseball cards, some paperback books, a stack of 45 rpm records, and a pile of eight-track tapes, but no candy.

"What can I do for you, Sheriff?" she asked when Rhodes made his way back to her through the crowded aisles. "Could I interest you in some baseball cards?" She tapped with a fingernail on the glass top of the candy counter. "I have a Jeff Bagwell rookie card here."

Michal was a short blond woman of indeterminate age. The first time Rhodes had seen her name on the window of her store, he'd thought it was misspelled, but she'd explained that it was the name of Saul's daughter in the Old Testament's Book of Samuel. Rhodes had never been much of a biblical scholar.

"I might have a Craig Biggio card, too," she added, "if you'd like to have a look at it."

"I gave up on baseball a long time ago," Rhodes said. "Before those two were even rookies."

"Maybe a nice forty-five, then. I have a couple by Elvis."

"I just wanted to ask a question," Rhodes said. "About your neighbor."

"Jamey the barber?"

"That's the one. Have you seen him today?"

"He was here this morning."

When she said the word morning, Rhodes realized that he'd missed lunch again. As soon as he realized it, his stomach felt hollow and empty.

"When did he leave?"

"Not long ago. Someone parked out in front of his shop

and went inside. After a few minutes, they both came back out and left."

"Do you know who it was?"

"No, but he was wearing a T-shirt that had 'I'm with Stupid' printed on the front."

"Bald, a little chubby, driving an old Ford pickup?"

"That's him. Is he in trouble?"

"No, and neither is Jamey—not yet anyway. There was something I wanted to tell him."

"Want me to take a message?"

Michal turned to a cabinet behind her and found a pencil and notepad.

"This isn't something I'd want you to tell him," Rhodes said. "I'll find him. Where does Jamey live?"

"Out in the country, about a mile past the rock crusher."

"I'll look for him there," Rhodes said. "Does he close up often?"

"Actually, he does. He has plenty of customers, though. He seems to be very fast at cutting hair, gets people out quickly. Maybe that's the secret to getting some time off."

"Maybe," Rhodes said.

He thanked Michal for her help and drove out to Hamilton's house. On the way, he passed the old college campus and main building that were located just off the highway. The building was nearly a hundred years old, but it was no longer a part of any college. It had been used for any number of things, most recently as a church, but the minister had left, and now the Clearview Players were converting it into a theater.

No one was working on the building when Rhodes drove by, and he wondered if the Clearview Players would change their name to the Obert Players if they ever got the theater completed and open for business.

When he passed the college building, Rhodes went by the

rock crusher at the edge of town. After that, the road wound through the countryside. In a normal year, it would have been shaded by trees whose limbs reached out over it and met in the middle. This year, the trees seemed shriveled and small, and there was only a little shade. Dead, dry leaves lay in the road and swirled aside as Rhodes drove over them.

Hamilton's house was small and had a nearly bare yard. Crawford's truck was parked in the shade of a chinaberry tree, but Rhodes didn't see another vehicle. When he knocked on the door, no one answered. He walked around the house and knocked on the back door. No answer there, either.

Something was going on, and Rhodes didn't know what it was. He didn't like that, but there was nothing he could do about it except drive back to Clearview. He was tempted to stop off and see how Ruth was doing, but she knew her job, and he didn't want to distract her.

He did, however, get onto the county road and head for C. P. Benton's house. The black mailbox by the road in front of the house had a little sign dangling from it. It said CASA DE MATH in red script. Rhodes wanted to talk to Benton, but the math teacher's Saturn was gone. Apparently, nobody Rhodes wanted to see was going to be home that day.

Rhodes pulled into the driveway. Benton's lawn might not have been mown in awhile, at least according to Judge Parry, but it was hard to tell because the grass was brown and dry. Benton obviously didn't believe in wasting water on something like grass. Rhodes didn't blame him. He didn't like mowing any more than Benton did.

The gardenia bush by the front door had a few late-summer blooms on it, white among the green leaves. At least Benton waters his plants, Rhodes thought as he backed up the car.

Rhodes drove to the highway. He decided to go to the college to see Benton. It was possible that Benton was there making some kind of preparation for the classes that would be starting in a week or so.

Max Schwartz's music store was on the way to the college, about a quarter of a mile from the college's new building. Rhodes saw Schwartz's red convertible parked in front, its top up. Next to it was a Saturn that had to belong to Benton. Rhodes flipped on his turn signal and pulled off the highway and into the parking lot.

Rhodes recalled that Benton had mentioned playing the guitar when he was doing the fighting crane pose, or whatever it was. Thinking it over, Rhodes wondered if Benton had been trying to impress Ruth Grady. Rhodes knew nothing much about Ruth's private life. He didn't think she was dating anybody. Rhodes thought it might be because a lot of men were intimidated by a woman who carried a pistol and worked for the sheriff's department. Somehow, however, he didn't think Benton was the type to be intimidated by anything.

At any rate, if Benton played guitar, it was perfectly natural that he might be at a music store that just happened to be owned by another member of his academy class. The fact that Benton was there didn't have to have anything at all to do with the destruction of the Crawfords' mobile home or the death of Terry Crawford.

It didn't have to have any connection to what the judge had warned Rhodes about earlier.

Vigilantes? It just wasn't possible.

FOUR

RHODES DIDN'T KNOW MUCH about guitars, but he did know the difference between an acoustic guitar and an electric one. Schwartz had several of both kinds hanging on the walls of his store. He also had posters advertising a variety of other instruments, which he no doubt hoped to sell to members of the Clearview Catamount marching band and stage band. The biggest poster of all didn't picture an instrument. It was an ad for a long-ago concert by the Kingston Trio, all the members of which were dressed in striped shirts.

Some kind of folk music came from a couple of big speakers on the walls, a song about a long black rifle. Rhodes didn't know if the song was by the Kingston Trio or not.

Schwartz's black Lab was asleep in a back corner. The music didn't seem to bother him, and he didn't even look up when Rhodes came in.

Schwartz wore a shirt similar to the ones in the Kingston Trio poster, but his was mostly pink, with gray stripes. He was middle-aged and had the spread to prove it, though his hair was still thick and black. He wore glasses with black plastic frames, the kind that Rhodes had last seen in a photograph of Buddy Holly.

Schwartz held an acoustic guitar and was showing C. P. Benton what might have been a chord. Rhodes wasn't sure. His musicianship wasn't any better than his biblical scholarship.

"Hey, Sheriff," Schwartz said when Rhodes came in. "I

was just teaching C.P. a song. 'Everglades' is the name of it. You know it?"

Rhodes shook his head, so Schwartz strummed a few bars and sang the words. Benton sang, too, keeping more or less to the tune in a rumbling bass. Rhodes thought that the song on the speakers might be causing him trouble.

"Turn off the music," Schwartz called to someone Rhodes couldn't see. "It's great, but it's interfering."

The music stopped after a couple of seconds. Benton and Schwartz started to sing again.

To Rhodes, what they sang sounded something like an old Everly Brothers song, though he couldn't have said which one. Maybe if Schwartz and Benton had been better singers, he could have figured it out.

When they were finished, Schwartz put the guitar down on a counter and said, "Benton tells me that the Crawfords' meth lab blew up."

"It was a mobile home," Rhodes said, looking at Benton. "Not a meth lab."

Schwartz looked contrite. "I should have said *alleged* meth lab. I've only been selling guitars for a year, and I've already forgotten all my legal training."

"You and Benton didn't happen to go out that way earlier today, did you?" Rhodes said.

"Why would I do that?" Schwartz asked, raising his eyebrows and furrowing his brow. "I hope you don't think I had anything to do with blowing up that meth—that *alleged* meth lab."

"It's about more than blowing things up," Rhodes said. "Terry Crawford's dead."

Benton, who had been looking at the guitar on the counter, turned around. He looked a little pale.

"I just told Max that the Crawfords were probably all right. I didn't know one of them was dead."

"He wasn't killed in the explosion," Rhodes said.

Schwartz's wife, Jackee, came into the room from the office in the back of the store. Her blond hair was cut short, and she had light blue eyes.

"Who wasn't killed?" she said.

"Terry Crawford," Benton told her. "But he *was* killed."

"Not in the explosion, though," Max said. "It happened some other way."

Jackee looked a little confused, and Rhodes didn't blame her. He said, "The Crawfords' mobile home blew up today. Terry was killed, but he didn't die in the mobile home."

"How did he die, then?"

"Somebody shot him."

Jackee nodded. "I'm not surprised."

She might not have been, but her answer gave Rhodes a little jolt.

"Why not?" he asked.

Jackee's eyes narrowed. "I don't want to talk about it."

Rhodes looked at Max, who shrugged. He didn't want to talk about it, either.

"This is a murder investigation," Rhodes said, though he wasn't absolutely certain. It was always possible that Crawford had shot himself. If that was the case, Ruth would find the gun and let Rhodes know. For the moment, he was treating the death as a homicide.

"Then I guess we'd better tell you," Max said. "The Crawfords like to think of themselves as guitar players. They were in some honky-tonk band when they were young, but I don't think they knew more than three chords."

"That's all you need," Benton said. "C, F, and G. They'll get you through nearly anything."

"Maybe you," Schwartz said. "Not a real player."

Benton looked hurt. "I write my own songs. Some of them are pretty good."

Schwartz didn't seem impressed. "Who says?"

"Everybody who's heard them."

"Your mother?"

"Actually, she doesn't like them very much."

Rhodes wondered just when he'd lost control of the interrogation he'd started. From just about the first sentence, he thought. He wondered if they were nervous, oblivious, or trying to distract him. That's what they might do if they were guilty of something.

"About the Crawfords," he said. "Remember them?"

Schwartz and Benton looked at him as if he'd just wandered in and interrupted their conversation. It was Jackee who spoke up.

"Those two came in one morning when Max wasn't here. They clowned around a little at first and then started talking about guitars and prices. I'm not much of a salesperson, but I told them what I knew. I could tell they weren't really interested. They joked around some more, and then they made some suggestive remarks."

Max's face reddened. "Nobody makes suggestive remarks to Jackee but me."

"And he doesn't make them all that often," Jackee said.

Rhodes thought she was trying to calm her husband with humor. "What did the Crawfords say?"

"It was Terry," Max said. His face was still red, and his hands were clenched at his sides. His voice was loud. "It's a good thing I wasn't here."

The noise woke the black Lab, which had slept through everything so far. The dog stirred around and lifted his head to see what was going on.

"Max," Jackee said. She put a hand on his arm.

Schwartz took a deep breath and let it out slowly. His hands unclenched.

"Sometimes I get a little carried away," he said. "I don't mean anything by it."

Jackee removed her hand. "Max is a softy down deep, but he doesn't like it when I'm threatened."

Somehow they'd moved from suggestive remarks to threats. Rhodes felt a little lost.

"'Threatened'?" he asked.

Back in the corner, the Lab lowered his head and closed his eyes.

"Let me start over," Jackee said. "The Crawfords came in. They looked at a couple of electric guitars, the cheapest ones we have."

Max pointed to a couple of guitars hanging on the wall. "Those little Johnson novice models aren't bad. Under a hundred and fifty dollars."

"You can get one at Wal-Mart for a lot less," Benton said.

"Sure, if you want something like that. These are cheap, but good."

"Never mind," Rhodes said. "Let her finish."

"I'm sorry," Benton said, but he didn't look sorry to Rhodes.

"I got one of the guitars and handed it to them," Jackee said. "They took it and asked me if I'd ever noticed how the body of a guitar was shaped like a woman. They started stroking it."

She stopped and looked at Max, but he was breathing normally, so she went on.

"You'd have to have been here," she said. "You'd have to have seen their faces, the way they looked at me."

"I can imagine," Rhodes said.

"Then one of them—maybe it was Terry; it's hard to tell them apart—said I must be here in the store alone a lot. He said he'd like to come for a visit sometime."

Rhodes assumed that was the threat she'd mentioned.

"That's when I came in," Max said. "I told the Crawfords to get out of here and not to come back."

"What did they say to that?" Rhodes asked.

"They said it was a free country. They said they'd come in whenever they wanted to."

"You know, you could have reported this to me."

"They didn't make any overt threats. They didn't say anything that couldn't be made to sound innocent if we'd tried to get a restraining order."

"Did they ever come back?"

"No," Schwartz said. "I told them that it was a free country all right and that if they ever came back, I was going to feel free to beat the hell out of them."

He stopped and looked at the floor, as if realizing that he might have said too much.

"He'd never do that, though," Jackee said. "They'd knock his glasses off, and he can't see three inches in front of him without them."

Rhodes looked over at the dog. "What about him?"

"He's lazy," Jackee said. "When he's awake, he loves everybody. He wouldn't hurt anybody, any more than Max would. The Crawfords could tell that about him. He lay there asleep the whole time."

"Max should learn the martial arts," Benton said, striking a pose. "I'm quite an expert myself."

"Really?" Schwartz said. "Where'd you learn? Watching old Chuck Norris movies?"

Benton appeared not to notice the sarcasm. "I learned from Shen Chuan at Professor Lansdale's school in Nacogdoches."

"I don't think Shen Chuan has all those funny poses."

"Well, I added those myself, to impress people and maybe avoid a fight. My body is a lethal weapon, and I don't want to hurt anybody if I don't have to."

"Really?"

"Really. I could teach you a few things."

"Too late," Rhodes said.

"Why's that?"

"Terry Crawford's already dead."

FIVE

AFTER HE LEFT the music store, Rhodes went back to the jail. Hack Jensen and Lawton, the jailer, already knew about Terry Crawford, thanks to Rhodes having called Ruth Grady to the crime scene. They would have dragged all the details out of Rhodes, but they had other things to talk about.

Unfortunately, even in a place as small and quiet as Blacklin County, there were things other than major cases that had to be dealt with. A man's death was important, and a terrible thing, but the sheriff's department couldn't stop and concentrate on that one thing. The regular crimes and annoyances demanded at least a little attention.

Hack could hardly wait to bring one of the annoyances to Rhodes's attention.

"Mikey Burns called," he said as soon as Rhodes came through the door.

Burns was the commissioner in whose district the Crawfords lived.

"What did he want?" Rhodes asked, knowing he'd never get a straight answer from Hack. The dispatcher and Lawton sometimes seemed to Rhodes to derive most of their pleasure in life by making him drag information from them. They had a physical resemblance to two comedians from the past, Bud Abbott and Lou Costello, but their act was a bit different.

"We're behind the times," Hack said. He was chubby but not

soft, and though he was well past normal retirement age, his hair was still black. "That's what it is."

Rhodes knew they were behind the times. They were supposed to have video cameras installed in all the county cars by now, but they didn't. Rhodes blamed the commissioners, who hadn't appropriated the money that he'd requested in the budget he'd prepared for them. The commissioners, on the other hand, blamed the taxpayers. Burns was the one who'd said the public wouldn't stand for any tax increases, so something had to be cut from the budget. For the last two or three years, the cut had been the video cameras.

"Is it the car cameras?" Rhodes asked.

"Nope," Lawton said. He was leaning against the wall by the door to the cell block. He was nearly as old as Hack, but thinner. He had a little mustache and slicked-back hair. "Not this time."

"You're gettin' warm, though," Hack said.

"A new crime lab?" Rhodes asked, knowing it was a ridiculous guess. The county crime lab was so primitive that they sent everything that needed to be analyzed or tested to the state lab, and the expense of bringing it up-to-date would be astronomical. Mikey Burns would never allow it. Even if he would, the county couldn't afford it. Supposedly, Burns had someone working on a federal grant proposal that would help out with funding, but Rhodes hadn't seen anything to prove it.

"That ain't it," Lawton said. "You're gettin' colder."

Hack turned and looked at Lawton, who was overstepping his authority in the game. As the dispatcher, Hack was the official purveyor of information, and he didn't like it when Lawton tried to cut in.

"It's the Web site," Rhodes said. "That's it, isn't it?"

Hack looked disappointed, as if the game had ended too soon, and Rhodes knew he was right.

"What did he say about it?" Rhodes asked.

"He said we were about the last department in the state without a Web site. He said he was gonna bring it up at the next meeting of the commissioner's court. He didn't say, but you know who he's gonna blame."

"The sheriff," Rhodes said.

"Remember, he didn't say that."

He didn't have to. Burns didn't much like Rhodes, and Rhodes didn't really blame him, considering what had happened to James Allen, Burns's predecessor in the precinct office. Allen had been Rhodes's friend for years, but that friendship had come to an end, along with Allen's tenure as a commissioner.

"We have a Web site," Rhodes said.

"Not accordin' to Burns. He says it's just a placeholder that's been up for a year. He says he wants action."

"He's the one who hired the Web site designer," Rhodes said. "He can't expect us to do the job ourselves."

"He says you're responsible for seein' that the job's done, and done right. He says—"

Rhodes didn't want to hear any more about what Burns had said. "The next time he calls, just tell him we have other things to worry about."

"He's not gonna call back. He wants to see you in his office today."

Having already taken a little chewing out from the county judge, Rhodes wasn't in the mood to talk to Burns. However, since Terry Crawford had been killed in Burns's precinct, and since Burns liked to know what was going on in his territory, Rhodes thought it would be a good idea to keep him informed. Besides, Burns held the purse strings. There was no use in antagonizing him any more than necessary.

"All right, I'll go talk to him," Rhodes said. "Give me a call if Ruth comes in. I want to talk to her as soon as she's finished with the crime scene."

"You tell Miz Wilkie we said hey," Lawton said as Rhodes started for the door.

Mrs. Wilkie had been Allen's secretary, and now she worked for Burns. At one time, she'd set her cap for Rhodes, but he'd married Ivy Daniel instead. Mrs. Wilkie had never quite forgiven him.

"She's a widow," Rhodes said to Lawton. "Maybe I could fix you two up."

For once, Lawton didn't have anything to say in reply. Hack was still laughing when Rhodes left.

A BACKHOE SAT in front of the precinct building, but the rest of the equipment was in the back in covered parking bays. The building itself was really just a big metal shed and workshop, with an office in front.

Mrs. Wilkie gave Rhodes a short nod when he came in. She typed a few more words at her computer and then said, "Good afternoon, Sheriff."

She was a formidable woman, but not one who'd ever done any work outside her home. Even after her husband had died, she'd remained a homemaker. After Rhodes had married Ivy, however, she had tried to change, and she'd been quite successful. A few years ago, Rhodes wouldn't have been able even to imagine her sitting at a typewriter, much less a computer.

"Good afternoon," he said. He thought it would be best if he didn't mention fixing her up with Lawton. "Is Commissioner Burns in?"

"Yes, and he's expecting you." Mrs. Wilkie smiled, as if she was pleased to think that Rhodes was being called on the carpet. "You can go right on in."

Rhodes went through the hollow-core door and into Burns's office. Burns sat at his desk, reading something on a piece of paper. He was balding, and the hair around the crown of his head was white. His eyes were blue, and he was always smiling, even when he was about to read the riot act to someone. He wore an aloha shirt, as he always did in the office. The one today was red, with yellow and green flowers.

For about half a minute, Burns continued to read, or to pretend to. Then he put down the paper and told Rhodes to have a seat.

Rhodes sat in a hard-bottomed chair across from Burns's desk while Burns fumbled through some more papers. Burns wasn't one of those men who kept a clean desk. Papers lay scattered all over. Some were folded, some were flat, and a couple were wadded into balls.

"Here we are," Burns said, pulling the piece he was looking for from under a small stack. "Let's talk about that Web site your department was supposed to have up and running"—he laid the paper down and put his finger at a point near the middle of it—"six months ago."

At least he didn't waste any time getting to the point, Rhodes thought.

"Melanie Muller's the one who was supposed to get it up and running," Rhodes said. "Not me."

"Don't go trying to shift the blame," Burns replied, raising his finger from the paper and pointing it at Rhodes. "You're the one responsible."

Rhodes didn't like people who pointed their fingers at him. He said, "You hired her."

Burns saw the way Rhodes was looking at him and lowered his hand. "Mel Muller's an expert at building Web sites. The best in Blacklin County."

Probably the *only* one in the county, Rhodes thought. "Maybe she's too busy to do our Web site. I gave her all the information and photographs long ago."

"Then you'd better check with her and see why she hasn't done it," Burns said.

Rhodes wondered why it was his job to do that, but he didn't want to antagonize Burns. He said he'd do it.

"And do it soon," Burns said. "We're lagging behind every county in the state, and I want us to have a sharp-looking Internet presence. Second to none."

Rhodes wondered if the words *Internet presence* had ever been spoken in a Blacklin County precinct barn before. He doubted it. He was about to tell Burns that he had a few other things he had to work on, including a possible homicide, but the commissioner didn't give him a chance.

"There's something else that's worrying me," Burns said. "I believe Judge Parry has already talked to you about it."

Rhodes nodded. "We had a meeting this morning."

"Then you know that some college professor's been causing trouble."

"Benton's his name," Rhodes said, "and he hasn't been causing any trouble. Someone has, though. Have you heard about Terry Crawford?"

"What about him?"

"He's dead," Rhodes said. "Somebody killed him. Or maybe he killed himself. It happened late this morning."

Burns leaned forward. "Why wasn't I told?"

"Because it's not your job to enforce the law here. Anyway, I'm telling you now."

"Whatever happens in my precinct is my concern. If somebody's been murdered because of your carelessness, then I want to know about it. That troublemaker—Benton—lives near the Crawfords. Did he have anything to do with it?"

"Deputy Grady is going over the crime scene now," Rhodes said, letting the remark about carelessness pass. "We don't know what happened or who might have been involved."

"I'll bet it was that Benton fella. He's a smart-ass, nosing around and asking questions all the time. That kind is always trouble."

"I'll keep you posted," Rhodes said, standing up. "I know you'd want me to take care of the investigation into Terry Crawford's death before anything else. You might want to give Ms. Muller a call."

Burns stood up, too. He looked uncomfortable. "That's going to be up to you."

Rhodes didn't know what to say to that, so he didn't say anything. He just stood there looking at Burns.

Burns looked away after a second or two.

"All right," he said, "I'll admit it. Mel's a little temperamental. She thinks she knows more than anybody else, and in this case, she does. She's a real prima donna. I don't think I can deal with her."

"But you recommended her."

"Because she's the best at what she does. She understands a computer better than anybody I've ever met. Being good with computers is a handy skill to have, but it can be a problem. Those creative types are always trouble, whether they're into painting or computers or music. Anything like that."

Rhodes grinned. "Dr. Benton plays guitar and writes his own songs."

Rhodes knew he shouldn't have said it, but he couldn't resist.

"I might have known," Burns said.

SIX

RHODES WAS ON HIS WAY to Melanie Muller's house when Hack called him on the radio.

"Ruth says you better get out to the Crawford place. She's got some things to show you."

"What things?" Rhodes asked.

"She didn't say," Hack told him.

Hack always wanted to be in the know, and Rhodes could hear the frustration in his voice.

"She probably didn't want it heard on the radio. Tell her I'll go right on out there."

Instead of going to visit Muller, Rhodes turned back toward the road to Obert. He would check on the Web site later—if he got around to it.

RUTH GRADY WAS WAITING at the well when Rhodes arrived. He left the car and went to meet her.

"What do you have?" he asked.

"Well, for one thing, it wasn't suicide. I didn't find any sign of a weapon."

Rhodes hadn't thought she would. Terry wasn't the suicidal type.

"I don't think Terry was shot down there where you found him," Ruth said. "Look."

She showed Rhodes a couple of spots in the dirt on the opposite side of the well. "I'm sure that's blood. I've taken some samples so we can compare it to Terry's. Now, look over here."

She led Rhodes to the trail through the grass. "I found a few more blood spots along the way. Luckily, we didn't step on them. I think that whoever shot Terry did it up here, maybe even in the house, but Terry got away. We won't find any blood close to the house because of the explosion and fire, though."

They wouldn't find any tracks that would help them, either. The ground had been too dry before the fire, and now that it was soaked, Ruth and Rhodes were the only ones who'd walked on it.

"Nobody followed Terry," Ruth said.

"How can you tell?"

"The path through the grass isn't trampled down enough. You and I followed along where Terry had gone and didn't get off the track, but if someone had been chasing him, he wouldn't have been so careful."

She and Rhodes looked at the trail again, and Rhodes had to agree with her.

"Did you find any ejected cartridges?" he asked.

"No. The killer either used a revolver or picked up the brass. Or maybe any brass he left was destroyed in the explosion. That's assuming that Terry was shot in the mobile home."

Rhodes wondered if that had been the case. If it was, why had the killer let Terry get away?

"Did you find anything else?"

"I didn't find any of the spent bullets. There might be one in Terry, but I don't know if that will help us any."

Rhodes would check with Dr. White after the autopsy about the bullets. He said, "And that's it? Nothing to help us find out who shot Terry?"

"You mean did Terry write the killer's name in the dirt before he died?"

"It would have been thoughtful of him," Rhodes said.

"How many times has that ever happened, that you know of?"

"I can't think of any."

"Well, this won't be the first time it's happened, either. Sorry about that."

"Did you find anything at all that might help?"

"You're talking about clues, right?"

"A clue would be nice."

"Nothing like that," Ruth said. "But I did find something interesting."

She's getting as bad as Hack and Lawton, Rhodes thought.

"Were you planning to tell me about it?"

"I'll do better than that. I'll show you."

They were standing near the spot where Rhodes had found Terry's body, and Ruth headed off to the right, toward the copse of trees.

"How far are we going?" Rhodes asked.

"Not far. Just inside the trees."

Rhodes should have known that Ruth would do a thorough investigation of the area. She hadn't stopped at Terry's body, but had gone over the whole place.

Sweat ran down Rhodes's sides under his shirt as they walked. Earlier in the day, he'd felt a little breeze, but there was no wind at all now. The dry grass and leaves were as still as if they'd been frozen stiff.

The woods were thicker than Rhodes had thought. The elms, oaks, pecans, and hackberries grew crowded together and made it hard to see much past the first line of them. Rhodes couldn't see anything that looked unusual or out of the ordinary.

As they walked, Rhodes asked, "What do you think about C. P. Benton?"

Ruth stopped abruptly. Rhodes stopped beside her.

"Why would I think about him?" she said.

Rhodes thought she might be blushing, but the redness of her face could have been just a result of the hot weather.

"I meant, what kind of person do you think he is," Rhodes told her. "Judge Parry thinks he's a troublemaker."

"He was really interested in the academy," Ruth said. "He's smart and kind of...odd."

"He seems interested in you," Rhodes said.

Ruth looked at him and he said, "It's not really any of my business."

"What do you mean by 'interested'?"

"You know." Rhodes wished he'd kept his mouth shut. "Like he might want to have a date with you."

"We'd better check out the woods," Ruth said. She started forward. "It's getting late."

Rhodes stayed beside her. "Right. What are we looking for?"

"It's over here," Ruth said.

She pointed to a gap in the trees. A narrow path led to it. Rhodes asked Ruth where the path came from, glad to be able to get back to business and off the topic of C. P. Benton.

"It comes from the top of the hill," Ruth said, "but it's pretty well hidden. A lot of it's in the trees. When the Crawfords came down here, they didn't want anybody to see them."

They walked on down to the gap, and Ruth went into the trees a little ahead of Rhodes, who smelled something strange but somehow familiar.

"There it is," Ruth said.

About fifteen yards ahead of them was a shed that covered a moonshine still.

Rhodes liked to watch old movies, usually awful ones, like *Alligator 2: The Mutation.* But now and then he'd watch something like *Thunder Road,* which the sight of the still immediately brought to mind. The daddy made the whiskey and the son drove the load, or something like that, according to the song that Robert Mitchum sang.

The Crawfords' still wasn't a big one, but it would make enough to keep their customers satisfied. Maybe about twenty gallons at a time. A copper boiler sat atop a brick furnace. Tubing ran from the top of it, coiling around and ending where a barrel or tub would have caught the finished product. The contraption was covered by the shed, which was concealed from the road by the trees and some camouflage netting that was strung over it. A couple of empty mash barrels stood nearby.

"Good grief," Rhodes said.

"It's a still," Ruth said. "Isn't it?"

Ruth was a good bit younger than Rhodes, and she'd probably never seen a still before, maybe not even a picture of one. Rhodes hadn't seen one in years himself.

"It's a still," he said. "No doubt about it."

"But what's it doing here?"

"You mean on this particular spot? They'd want it close to the creek so they could get the water, and they'd want it in the trees to keep it hidden."

"I meant why is it here at all? Do people still drink moonshine whiskey?"

"Sure they do," Rhodes said, going on to explain the demand for it.

Blacklin County was dry in the sense that only beer and wine could be sold there. People who wanted the hard stuff had to drive a few miles to another county, and there were some who might not like to drive that far. Others would believe that 'shine was superior to any commercial brew. Some might even drink it because it had more of a kick.

The superiority was what appealed to a wider market. Sales of 'shine in the cities around the state had been booming in a couple of different strata of society. High rollers from the old-money families liked to buy it to show off for their friends at parties. People with new money, mostly in some area of the entertainment business, liked the novelty of it. They were willing to pay a premium for the good stuff.

"So there would be a good market," Ruth said, "if you could get the whiskey to them."

"I don't think the Crawfords could do that," Rhodes said. "They're small-time, and so's this still. They could sell some product here in the county, though, which explains the cars that C. P. Benton saw around here."

"They didn't come here for meth," Ruth said. "They were looking for another kind of drug."

"That's right, and it explains why the Crawford boys didn't look like meth users themselves."

They might have used some of their product, Rhodes thought, and they probably had, but drinking whiskey wouldn't be nearly as detectable at a glance as if they'd been hitting the crystal.

"How does it work?" Ruth asked. "The still, I mean."

"You mix corn chops and sugar in water and let it rot for a while. That gives you the sour mash that you run through the still. You can add some ingredients if you want to—apples, oak chips, potatoes, whatever. I hear that some people used to add Dr Pepper."

"You might like that," Ruth said.

"I prefer my Dr Pepper straight. Anyway, after that, you cure it out in charred oak barrels if you're going for the best brew you can make. Otherwise, you just start selling it. I figure the Crawfords were going for the good stuff."

"It doesn't look as if they've fired the thing up recently," Ruth said.

"Probably not since the creek's been low," Rhodes replied. "Unless they got the water from somewhere else."

Ruth looked at the still for a couple of seconds. "People brew beer at home, and that's legal. Why not whiskey?"

"Taxes," Rhodes said. "It's always been about taxes. And then there's the other little problem."

"What problem?"

"Home brew can kill you, or at least make you pretty sick, if there's a problem with it. Sometimes the first and last parts of a batch will be toxic."

"Didn't the federal agents break these things up with axes back in the old days?"

"Revenuers," Rhodes said. "That's what they were called. They did use axes sometimes."

"Maybe we'd better get us a couple."

"We'll leave it for the time being. The state boys will want to see it. Nobody's going to use it now, and it'll be evidence against Larry Crawford."

"Better not leave it too long. With the price of copper these days, it's probably worth more than the whiskey. Somebody's likely to come carry it off."

She had a point. Lately, there had been a whole series of thefts involving copper: coils stolen from air conditioners, wiring stripped out of vacant houses, water pipes from construction sites. Most of the thefts were related to drugs, primarily meth. People needed quick cash, and copper was a way to get it. No doubt most of the Crawfords' customers knew approximately where the still was located.

"Have you taken pictures?"

"Yes. I did that when I found it."

"Good," Rhodes said. "We'll be sure to padlock the gate when we leave. That'll have to do."

Ruth nodded. "What about Larry Crawford? Are you going to arrest him?"

"I am if I can find him," Rhodes said. "He's disappeared."

He told Ruth about his visit to Obert and to Jamey Hamilton's house.

"So he doesn't even know his brother's dead," Ruth said.

"That's right. I wanted to let him know, but I couldn't locate him."

For some reason, Rhodes thought of *Thunder Road* again. In the movie, the law didn't get the moonshiners because the devil got them first, or so the song said. Somebody had already gotten Terry—the devil, or vigilantes, or someone. Rhodes didn't much blame Larry for hiding.

"He's got to be around the county somewhere," Ruth said.

"We'll see," Rhodes replied. "It's getting late. We'd better get back to town. You need to write up your report."

They started out of the woods. As soon as they got to the edge of the trees, Rhodes heard the sound of an engine.

Ruth heard it, too, and they both stopped.

"Maybe you should have padlocked that gate sooner," Ruth said.

If he'd done that, as Ruth well knew, they'd both have needed a key to the padlock that Chief Parker had given Rhodes, and Rhodes had only one. Parker had kept the other.

"We'll just have to tell whoever it is to leave," Rhodes said. He started up the hill.

He'd gone about thirty yards when he saw a black pickup crest the hill and start down toward him. For a second or two, Rhodes didn't think anything of it. He assumed the driver would see him, the truck would stop, and he'd find out what was going on.

It didn't work out like that. The truck's engine roared, and its big tires churned up the dust and weeds, throwing them in the air behind it. It picked up speed. Grasshoppers flew up in front of it like popping corn, and the driver aimed the bumper right at Rhodes.

A brush guard was mounted in front of the bumper. It was

a cast-iron monstrosity supposedly designed to shove brush aside and protect the front of the truck.

Rhodes thought it would also do a fine job of protecting the truck from any unwary sheriff who happened to be in the way. It would shove him aside like a pesky mesquite.

Unlike the pesky mesquite, which would bounce right back, Rhodes would probably suffer several breaks, bumps, and bruises; and he wouldn't be bouncing back quickly, if he bounced at all.

Rhodes waved his arms to get the driver's attention. The truck didn't change course. Apparently, Rhodes already had the driver's attention, and that was too bad for Rhodes.

The setting sun glared off the truck's windshield, so Rhodes couldn't see the driver. The front license plate was missing. Lots of people who lived outside of town kept old trucks around to use on their property, and since they never took them anywhere else, they didn't bother to register them. The truck was old all right—maybe twenty years old, maybe more than that. The only identifier Rhodes could see on this one was the ram's head sitting on the front of the hood, so the truck was a Dodge.

Rhodes didn't like to carry a sidearm. He thought that if he carried one, he'd be tempted to use it. Nevertheless, he was armed. He'd tried several kinds of holsters over the years, and he'd never been satisfied with any of them. He was currently using an ankle holster, and by the time he bent down, pulled up his pants, and pulled out the pistol, he'd either be bumped aside or flattened.

Ruth was behind him, and she had a pistol in a belt holster. Rhodes decided to get out of her way and let her stop the truck. As for him, he was going to run.

Rhodes didn't like to run even in the best of conditions. He especially didn't like to run through weeds and mesquite bushes when it was hot. And he liked it considerably less under these conditions, when a big black truck was chasing him.

As soon as he broke to the left, the truck swerved to follow. He ran ten or twelve yards. The mesquite thorns tore at him when he got too close to the bushes. They ripped his shirt and scraped his hands.

He stopped and turned around. The truck changed directions, too.

Rhodes glanced at Ruth Grady. She had a two-handed grip on her pistol and was ready to fire, but Rhodes kept getting in her way.

It wasn't his fault. The driver was doing an admirable job of keeping Rhodes between her and the truck.

Rhodes did what he should have done to begin with. He turned and headed back to the trees.

Ruth snapped off a couple of shots when Rhodes passed her. He assumed she was shooting for the tires, but he didn't hear them burst.

The truck was almost on her then, and she turned and followed Rhodes. He was going all out, but Ruth passed him handily.

He didn't turn around to see where the truck was. He didn't have to. He could tell by the sound of the engine that it was almost on top of him. He imagined he could feel the heat coming off the radiator.

The trees were right in front of him.

Rhodes jumped for them.

SEVEN

RHODES FLEW BETWEEN an elm and a pecan tree, hit the ground, rolled, and banged his head into the trunk of another elm. His nose hurt, and he smelled dirt and tasted grit.

The largest trees are plenty big enough to stop the truck, he thought as he lay there. At least he hoped they were. Maybe the driver would have sense enough to stop.

He didn't. The crash splintered some of the thinner tree trunks, and Rhodes heard them crack. He sat up to look for Ruth and saw that the truck was backing up to make another try at breaking through to him.

His head throbbed as he pulled up his pants leg and reached for the .38 in the ankle holster. He ripped the Velcro flap up and jerked the pistol free. He didn't try to hit the truck's tires, which he couldn't see anyway. He fired at the windshield.

The first bullet whanged off the brush guard, but the second punched through the windshield, starring the glass.

The truck engine stopped roaring for a second. When it started again, the truck was rushing up the hill in reverse. Rhodes knew he couldn't catch up with it, so he put his pistol back into the holster, smoothed down the flap, and looked around for Ruth.

She sat with her back against a tree trunk, holding her left wrist. "I think I sprained it," she said. "Who were those guys?"

Rhodes didn't have any idea. "Whoever it was, they didn't much like us."

"Your nose is bleeding," Ruth told him.

Rhodes wished that he, like C. P. Benton, carried a hand-kerchief. Since he didn't, he wiped off his upper lip with the back of his hand. He felt dirt and grit on his face, and his nose was tender.

"Can you stand up?" he asked Ruth.

"It's my wrist that hurts," she said, getting to her feet. "And my pride, a little. I hated to run."

Rhodes remembered his high school English class again and something about discretion being the better part of valor. Shakespeare, he thought, but not something he'd had to memorize. If he remembered it anyway, maybe he'd been a better student than he'd thought. His teacher would have been proud of him. If he was right, that is.

"I hate running, too," he said, brushing off some of the dirt, dead leaves, and sticks that clung to his pants and shirt. "But sometimes it's the best thing to do unless you want to get flat-tened by a truck."

"I'd like to know who was driving and where he came from."

Rhodes told her about the license plate.

"Attempted murder," Ruth said. She brushed at her clothing with one hand. "Premeditated."

"He might not have come here to kill us," Rhodes said. "He could have been after the copper."

"Or maybe he came for something else. We need to look around a little better."

"What about your wrist?"

"I'll be all right. Come on."

Instead of leaving the woods, she started back through the trees, heading in the direction of the still. Rhodes wondered what she had in mind, and then it occurred to him that maybe the Crawford brothers hadn't sold all their 'shine. Maybe some of it was hidden nearby.

That was Ruth's idea, too. When they got to the still, she said, "I should have looked around here more carefully."

"Finding the still was good enough. There wasn't any reason to think there'd be anything else around."

"Now there is," Ruth said.

Rhodes knew her wrist must be hurting, but she didn't mention it. She moved the mash barrels, using her good hand, and looked beneath them.

Rhodes checked the ground around the still. He found a place where the dirt was loose rather than packed and hard. He scraped at it with his foot. It didn't take him long to uncover a board. He had a shovel in the county car, but he didn't want to walk back up the hill and get it, so he kept on scraping with his foot until he'd uncovered the edges of several boards. A couple of crosspieces held them together.

Bending over, Rhodes took hold of the boards, then lifted them up. In the hole that he uncovered were five one-gallon jugs of what had to be moonshine.

"That's what he was after," Ruth said, standing beside Rhodes and looking down at the clear liquid in the bottles. "Maybe the copper, too."

Rhodes wasn't entirely convinced. He thought the driver might have been after him and Ruth. I'll find out, he told himself.

"This Jamey Hamilton you mentioned," Ruth said, "does he drive a truck?"

"I don't know. We'll have to check. Why? Do you think Crawford came back for the liquor?"

Ruth shrugged, then winced. "He could have. That wasn't his truck, though."

"You'd better go on back to town," Rhodes said. "Stop by the ER and have somebody take a look at that wrist. You can write your report later, when you're feeling better."

"I'm fine. What are we going to do with this whiskey?"

"It's evidence, so we'll confiscate it. I'll take it to the jail and put it in the evidence room. You go on by the hospital and then go home."

"All right," Ruth said.

AFTER RUTH LEFT, Rhodes walked around over the area where the black truck had driven to see if he could find a clue. He didn't really think the license plate would have fallen off, though it would have cheered him up if it had. He just hoped he'd find something that would help him identify the truck.

He didn't. He just got hotter and sweatier.

After awhile, he gave up and went to the county car. He drove down to the edge of the woods and loaded the whiskey in the trunk, doing his best not to smear any fingerprints that might be on the jars.

When he left the property, he chained the gate and put the padlock on the chain. If the driver of the black truck was after the whiskey or the still, he'd have to cut the fence to get back onto the place. That wouldn't be a difficult job, and for that matter, he could just drive right through the gate with that brush guard on the front of the truck. Well, Rhodes thought, at least the gate, or even the fence, would slow him down some. Somehow, it wasn't a very satisfying thought. The fire department had bolt cutters for chains, and the driver of the pickup could have them, too.

It was getting on toward evening, and Rhodes still hadn't talked to Melanie Muller. He figured it might be a good idea to do that before he went back to the jail, so he drove by her house when he got to town.

Actually, she didn't live in a house. She lived in what people liked to call "a manufactured home," which, as far as Rhodes could see, was like a mobile home that you couldn't run a set of wheels under and drive off the property. It was on the edge of town, on the road to Milsby, a little town that no longer existed in any meaningful sense. Mrs. Wilkie lived out that way, too.

The house had no garage, but a late-model tan Chevrolet sat on a short gravel driveway. Rhodes parked behind the Chevy, got out, and went to the door. To get to it, he had to climb a set of wooden steps that had been bought ready-made and shoved in front of the manufactured home. On either side of the steps were neat flower beds with a couple of rosebushes in each, but no roses were blooming.

His knock was answered by a short blond woman wearing a man's work shirt and jeans. She had on a pair of half glasses, like the ones Rhodes used for reading, and she took them off and put them in her shirt pocket.

"Yeah?" she said.

"I'm Sheriff Dan Rhodes. I wanted to talk to you about the Web site you're doing for our department."

"I was just about to have supper."

Rhodes wasn't going to let her off that easily.

"Sorry to interrupt. I won't keep you long."

"Well, all right. Come on in. I was just going to have chili from a can anyway."

That didn't sound bad to Rhodes, who hadn't had chili in a good while, from a can or otherwise. Ivy was trying to get him to eat healthy food, which was hard to get used to after years of baloney sandwiches. Healthy food just wasn't as satisfying somehow. Rhodes cheated now and then, but when he did, he didn't mention it to Ivy.

"With beans?" he asked.

Muller looked at him quizzically. "No, without. Why?"

"I like it with beans."

"Real chili fans don't eat beans, not with chili."

"I know. It's a personal failing."

"That figures. Well, don't just stand there. Come on inside."

Muller moved back from the door and Rhodes went into a small living area with a couch, TV set, a low coffee table, and an easy chair. The coffee table was covered with computer magazines. A couple lay on the floor under it, and a couple more were in the easy chair.

Glancing through the doorway on the opposite side of the room, Rhodes saw a dining table and a refrigerator. On his right, another door opened into an office with a couple of computer desks, each holding a computer with a screen saver flickering. On the wall there was a big poster of Alvin and the Chipmunks. Alvin was in the middle, wearing a red baseball cap and a red sweater with a big yellow A on it. Simon and Theodore stood on either side of him. Rhodes didn't know which was which. One of them was taller and wore glasses, but that was no help.

"Did you come here to talk or just to admire the artwork?" Muller said.

Rhodes turned to her. "I was wondering which one was Simon. I can never keep the chipmunks straight."

"Simon's the one with the glasses."

"Thanks. Maybe I can remember that."

Muller gave him a skeptical look, as if to say she doubted it. Rhodes thought she might ask him to sit down, but she didn't.

"Get on with it," she said.

Rhodes was beginning to see what Burns had meant when he'd said she was "difficult."

"Mikey Burns wanted me to stop by and see what kind of progress you're making on the Web site," he said.

She looked him over, as if seeing him for the first time.

"You couldn't have cleaned up first?"

Her gaze made Rhodes acutely conscious of the fact that he'd recently been rolling around in leaves and dirt and that he could probably use a good bath. He was beginning to wish he'd skipped the visit.

"I didn't want to wait," he said. "Mr. Burns wants a report tomorrow."

"He couldn't have called me?"

Rhodes recalled his high school English class again. His teacher was always asking questions that he didn't have answers for. So he did what he'd done in high school. He made something up.

"He thought a personal visit would be better."

"Then why didn't he come by himself?"

"The Web site's not for him or the precinct, just the sheriff's department. He thought I'd be a better representative than he would."

This time, Muller didn't ask a question. She just looked at Rhodes in a way that let him know the department would have been better off sending someone considerably spiffier.

"What can I tell him?" Rhodes said.

"You can tell him that it takes time to create a professional Web site. You can tell him that I'm working on it. You can tell him that he should come by himself if he wants answers to his questions."

She stopped. Rhodes waited. She kept quiet.

"Fine," he said after a couple of seconds. "But what about a date when it might be ready? Can I give him a date?"

"He wouldn't know what a date was if it bit him in the butt," Muller said. "Are you through now?"

Rhodes supposed that he was. He thanked her for her time and drove to the jail.

EIGHT

WHEN RHODES PARKED in front of the jail, the first thing he saw was the black Infiniti. He wondered what Randy Lawless would be doing there, and he supposed there was only one way to find out. He got out of the big Ford and went inside.

"Good evening, Sheriff," Lawless said when Rhodes came through the door. "You're looking sharp tonight."

Rhodes wasn't fond of sarcasm. "So are you," he said, but in Lawless's case, it was true.

Lawless sat in one of the visitors' chairs, looking cool, calm, and relaxed. He wore a dark blue suit with a clean white shirt and a striped tie that probably cost more than Rhodes's whole outfit. For that matter, he probably spent more on aftershave every year than Rhodes spent on clothing.

"Mr. Lawless is here to talk to you about his client," Hack said, grinning.

"What client would that be?" Rhodes asked.

Hack probably hoped that Lawless wouldn't say. That way Rhodes would be forced to draw the information out of Hack, a process that could take a long time.

Lawless wasn't in on the joke, however, and said, "Larry Crawford."

Hack's grin was replaced by a look of disappointment.

Rhodes crossed the room to his desk and sat down. "That's interesting," he said. "Why does Larry need a lawyer? Has he been engaging in any criminal activity? Maybe he'd like to come in and make a full confession."

"No criminal activity," Lawless said. "And not a confession. That's not why I'm here."

Hack jumped in before Lawless could go any further. "He's here about the lawsuit Larry's going to file."

Rhodes was feeling lost, which he knew was exactly what Hack wanted. He said, "Lawsuit?"

"That's right," Lawless said. "He's going to file more than one, I think, and we'd like to cooperate with you and Chief Parker in the investigations you'll be doing on the explosion that destroyed Larry's home."

Rhodes understood exactly what Lawless was saying. More than that, he understood exactly what Lawless *meant,* which was that he'd want Rhodes and Parker to hand over the results of their investigations to him to use in his lawsuits, whatever those were. But there was more to it than that.

"You can get a police report," Rhodes said. "Just like anybody else."

"Of course," Lawless said, smiling, and Rhodes knew he wasn't going to say any more.

Rhodes looked at Hack, but the old dispatcher didn't have anything to add this time. They both knew that Lawless hoped Rhodes would do all his work for him, or most of it. Then the lawyer could pay a few dollars for the police report, get his investigations done for next to nothing, and charge his client big bucks.

The only catch that Rhodes could see was that Crawford, as far as Rhodes knew, didn't have big bucks. While natural-gas wells were being drilled all over the county, no gas had been found in the vicinity of Crawford's property. And while the sales of the Crawfords' homemade hooch might have been brisk, they almost certainly hadn't made Crawford rich.

"Who's paying you?" Rhodes asked. "I know Crawford can't afford your rates."

"I'm taking his case on a contingency basis," Lawless said.

The conversation was getting as bad as one with Hack and Lawton. Rhodes still wasn't clear about just what the lawsuit was all about. He said, "What case?"

Hack jumped in again. "Wrongful death."

"Ah," Rhodes said.

Now he knew what was going on. As Lawless might put it, he "should have known" sooner. He wondered, however, if Lawless knew what had happened to Terry Crawford. It didn't seem likely, since Hack wasn't the type to give out information freely, if at all, and even Hack didn't know about the still. However, you never could tell what someone like Lawless might have been able to find out somehow or other.

"Crawford will be suing the manufacturer of the propane unit," Lawless said. "If that's what caused the explosion today, that is. And possibly the installers. Maybe the propane distributors, too, and the people who built the house, as well."

It made sense to Rhodes, or it would have if he'd been a lawyer. Why leave anybody out? Manufacturers of propane tanks were supposed to make certain that their tanks and pipes were safe and didn't leak. The people who installed the systems were to be sure of the same things. The distributor, or whoever provided the propane, was responsible for the odorant that gave the ordinarily odorless gas a distinctive smell so leaks could be detected before there was an accident, like an explosion.

"Are you representing Crawford in anything else?" Rhodes asked.

Lawless shifted in his chair. He looked a little less relaxed. "For instance?"

Hack perked up.

"I was just curious," Rhodes said. "No charges have been filed or anything like that. When did Larry come to you about this lawsuit of his?"

Lawless didn't answer for a couple of seconds. "That might be confidential."

"I said that no charges have been filed. It's just that I went looking for your client this afternoon and couldn't find him."

"What did you want with him?"

"I wanted to tell him that his brother was dead."

"Oh," Lawless said, relaxing again. "He already knows that."

Rhodes looked at Hack, who shook his head.

"So what you're implying," Rhodes said, looking back at Lawless, "is that Larry believes his brother was killed in an explosion at their mobile home and that the explosion was caused by a faulty propane tank."

"Not exactly," Lawless said. "But that's close enough for now. You have any problems with that?"

Hack grinned broadly. Rhodes knew how much it pleased him to have key information that another person didn't.

"Why don't you tell him, Hack," Rhodes said.

"Well now, I don't think it's my place," Hack said.

"Tell me what?" Lawless said.

Rhodes crossed his arms and leaned back in his chair. "About Terry Crawford."

"What about Terry?"

"He's dead," Hack said, playing his favorite game. Rhodes was almost ashamed for helping him, but not ashamed enough to stop.

Lawless nodded. "We've established that."

"Nope," Hack said. "You're overlookin' one little thing."

"What?"

"The body."

"Oh, of course. Larry told me that the body hadn't been found yet. He's sure it will be once the fire department does a full investigation. Terry was in the mobile home when Larry left."

"He ain't there now," Hack said.

That got Lawless's attention. "He's not?"

"Nope. He's here in town."

"In town?" Lawless was clearly puzzled. "I thought you said he was dead. Are you telling me he's alive?"

Rhodes smiled. He didn't like it when Hack played this game with him, but he enjoyed seeing Lawless squirm a little. He knew it was wrong, but he couldn't help himself.

"Yes and no," Hack said. "Yes, he's in town, and no, he's not alive."

Lawless had never gotten flustered in court, or if he had, Rhodes hadn't heard about it. He was, however, getting a little flustered now.

"So the fire department's already found the body?"

"Nope," Hack said.

As Rhodes knew all too well, Hack could have gone on like that for hours. It was too bad that Lawton wasn't there to enjoy it and help out.

"Dammit," Lawless said, moving to the edge of the chair and leaning forward. "Can't you ever just say what you mean?"

Rhodes thought that was a fine comment for a lawyer to make, and he flashed back yet again to his high school English class, remembering what his teacher had said about irony.

"I always say what I mean," Hack said. "That's what I've been doin'."

Rhodes decided that he'd better interrupt before things got any worse.

"What Hack's telling you in his own roundabout way," Rhodes said, "is that Terry's dead all right, but he didn't die in the explosion of the mobile home."

"How do you know that?"

"Because I found his body. You might still have a wrongful death suit, though."

"And I hope you're going to tell me why."

"Because Terry Crawford was murdered," Rhodes said.

LAWLESS HADN'T STAYED AROUND for long after Rhodes's revelation. Although Rhodes had tried to get him to talk about when Crawford had engaged him and what time he'd left Lawless's office, the lawyer was vague and unhelpful.

Rhodes had also asked where Crawford was staying, but Lawless claimed not to know that, either.

"Did he mention his cousin?" Rhodes asked. "Jamey Hamilton?"

"He may have," Lawless said. "I don't remember."

Rhodes didn't quite believe that. "The next time you see your client, you tell him I want to talk to him."

"I don't know when that might be," Lawless said. "We don't have a meeting set up."

"You could give him a call."

"I don't have his cell number."

Rhodes didn't believe that, either, but he let Lawless leave without pushing him too far. When the lawyer was gone, Hack started in on Rhodes.

"What were you asking all those questions for?" he said. "And why're you all scuffed up like you are? You been playin' in a sandpile? Where's Ruth? Is she all right?"

Rhodes would have answered him, but just then Lawton came in from the cell block.

"What we need," Lawton said, "is a new jail, one of them modern ones where you can watch all the inmates on TV and don't have to go check on 'em all the time." He looked at Rhodes. "You been in a fight?"

"He won't tell me," Hack said. "He's keepin' it all to himself."

"I'll tell you all about it," Rhodes said. "Just as soon as I get all that whiskey out of the county car."

"Whiskey?" Hack said.

"What whiskey?" Lawton asked.

Rhodes just smiled.

NINE

LAWTON HELPED RHODES put the 'shine in the evidence room. Hack had to stay at his desk and answer the calls. Rhodes could tell that it was killing them not to ask any more questions, but they managed to keep quiet, because Rhodes had threatened not to tell them a thing if they didn't.

When the evidence was secured and labeled, Rhodes sat down at his desk and went through the whole thing for them.

"So the Crawford boys were runnin' 'shine," Hack said. "I bet they had plenty of customers who'll be gettin' mighty nervous about now."

"We won't be arresting anybody on the Crawfords' say-so," Rhodes told him. "So nobody has anything to be nervous about—yet. Buying the booze isn't the problem unless you're caught in the act. Making it's the problem. But not ours."

"You gonna call in the TABC?"

The TABC was the Texas Alcoholic Beverages Commission, the agency assigned to deal with bootlegging, among other things, which included prostitution, gambling, weapons, and narcotics. They'd have been involved in the meth lab if the Crawfords had been running one.

"I'll call them tomorrow," Rhodes said.

"You didn't mention any whiskey to Lawless."

"Son of a gun. I must have forgotten."

"Yeah," Hack said. "I noticed your memory's gettin' bad lately. Won't the TABC be ticked that you brought in the 'shine?"

"Can't help it if they are," Rhodes said. "It's evidence, and somebody might have taken it off."

"Somebody's nervous all right," Lawton said. "Prob'ly lookin' for that booze. Else they wouldn't be tryin' to run you and Ruth down."

"We need to find out who owns that truck," Rhodes said to Hack. "When Buddy comes in tomorrow, you tell him to talk to the Dodge dealers in all the counties around here and see if any of them remember that brush guard. Anyway, if that truck's as old as it looked to me, that's not a dealer-installed item."

"Most likely somebody installed that himself," Hack said. "On an old truck like that, it's prob'ly a custom job."

"Maybe got a welder to do it," Lawton added.

"Have Buddy check around with welders, too, then."

Rhodes didn't think a pickup that distinctive could be hidden easily, not with a bullet hole through the windshield, but all the driver would have to do would be to remove the brush guard and go to a city like Houston and get the windshield replaced. So the best bet would be to find someone who remembered it and might know who owned it. Which reminded Rhodes to tell Hack to send a deputy to the courthouse first thing in the morning and find out what kind of vehicles were registered in Jamey Hamilton's name.

The truck might not have been registered at all, but there was a chance the license plate had been removed. Rhodes wanted to be sure.

"I'll send Buddy," Hack said.

"You'd better have him check on stolen vehicles, too," Rhodes said.

"You got any ideas who killed Terry?" Hack said after he wrote himself a note or two.

"Not yet."

"What about Ruth? She gonna be all right?"

Hack hadn't been fond of Ruth when she'd first come to

work in the department. He hadn't liked the idea of a woman deputy around the jail. Ruth had won him over quickly, however, and now they were friends..

"She'll be fine. It's just a sprained wrist."

"Could be broke," Lawton said. "Hard to tell sometimes."

"She'll get it taken care of. They'll take X-rays if there's any question. She'll be in tomorrow. You tell her to fingerprint those whiskey jars. We might get lucky."

"I'll tell her," Hack said. "What about you? You okay?"

"Nothing wrong with me that a bath and something to eat won't take care of."

"You better get on home, then. You got a big day comin' up tomorrow."

"I don't think I'll have time for anything tomorrow," Rhodes said. "I have a murder investigation going on."

"Be good publicity for the book," Lawton said.

"I don't think Terry would look at it that way."

"Prob'ly not," Hack said.

AS RHODES DROVE HOME, he thought about the big day Hack had mentioned. A few years earlier, Jan and Claudia, a couple of women from out of town, had attended a writers' workshop that had been held on the old college campus out at Obert. They'd intended to write a true-crime book or something of the sort, and they'd come back to the county to do some research while Rhodes was working on another case.

It turned out that the material they collected was better suited to a novel, or maybe they were better suited to writing fiction than fact. At any rate, they'd written a novel about, as they put it, "a handsome crime-busting sherrif," and it had been accepted and published. Jan and Claudia would be at the Clearview Wal-Mart the next day for their first book signing, and they'd asked Rhodes to be there, too.

Claudia and Jan were also the two "outside agitators" that Rhodes had thought of when he was talking to Judge Parry. When they'd heard about the Citizens' Sheriff's Academy, they'd applied, even though they didn't live in the county. Rhodes had lobbied to get them in, even though there were some residents who then had to be left off the list to accommodate them.

Parry hadn't been happy about that, but Rhodes had persuaded him it was a good idea. He'd argued that if the book was a success, the two women might write others and get the county some favorable national press.

All that had been before Rhodes had read the book. Actually, he still hadn't read it, but he'd read the manuscript. The book was called *Blood Fever,* and sure enough, there was a handsome crime-busting sheriff.

But the character was nothing like Rhodes. His name was nothing so ordinary as Dan. It was Sage Barton. Sage was a bachelor who got up at five o'clock in the morning for a breakfast of Cheerios and fruit. He then spent some quality time with his cat, a black neutered tom named Satan, before he went out and jogged four miles through the quiet streets of the small town where he lived.

After that, and over the course of three hundred or so pages, Sage caught a bank robber after a running gun battle, discovered that a serial killer was at work in the county, had a steamy romance with a beautiful FBI profiler named Jennifer, uncovered the serial killer's grisly secret, was captured, then rescued by the beautiful profiler, who was then nabbed by the killer, who fled with her to his underground lair, where, after a car chase that had covered several chapters, Sage Barton cornered the killer for a final battle that involved fists, knives, feet, teeth, and, unless Rhodes was misremembering, a pair of nunchucks.

According to Jan and Claudia, the sheriff was based on Rhodes and the book on their experiences in Blacklin County.

Rhodes had a little trouble seeing the similarities. He did, he had to admit, have a cat, but that was about it. And he'd acquired the cat only recently. Jan and Claudia had never seen it and hadn't even known about it when they were writing the book.

So while he supposed he was flattered to be the model for a character in a book, he didn't see that the story had any connection to reality, and he was pretty sure the book wasn't going to bring the county the kind of publicity the judge would approve of.

The truth was that Blacklin County, which covered around a thousand square miles, was a sparsely populated area. Rhodes figured there weren't more than 25,000 people living there, and that was probably a high estimate. If a serial killer started working in the county, he'd halve the population in a few days. The last bank robbery Rhodes could recall had happened more than twenty years earlier, before he'd been elected sheriff.

As for gun battles, Rhodes hadn't taken part in one in awhile, though he'd been in a pretty good firefight in a cemetery a few years ago. That probably didn't count, since he hadn't been moving around much. Most of the time, he'd been hiding behind the biggest tree he could find.

And steamy romance? Rhodes had married Ivy Daniel after his first wife had been dead for a number of years, but their courtship couldn't have been described as steamy. Rhodes wasn't the steamy sort.

When he'd mentioned these things to Jan and Claudia, they'd told him that they didn't matter.

"What we wanted to do was tell a good story," Jan said.

"One with a little action in it," Claudia added. "The last time we were here, the major crime news was that a pizza parlor didn't have a sneeze guard over the salad bar."

That wasn't true. They had been there when Rhodes had

solved a murder that had occurred years before. He thought that was a pretty interesting case.

"It lacked car chases," Jan said.

"And gunfights," Claudia added.

"Not to mention a serial killer," Rhodes said. "And romance."

The women nodded. Claudia said, "We want to sell some books, so we exaggerated a little."

"Poetic license," Jan said. "You know."

Rhodes didn't know, but he got the idea. Now that the two women had been in the academy, their next book would probably feature a terrorist attack on rural Texas, so the sheriff could have a steamy romance with a beautiful member of Homeland Security.

Rhodes was glad he had a good excuse not to go to the book signing.

WHEN RHODES GOT HOME, Ivy gave him a look he'd become familiar with. It seemed to say, What on earth have you been up to?

So he told her. It had taken her awhile to get used to the fact that now and then he was going to be in dangerous situations, and she still didn't like the idea.

"So someone murdered Terry Crawford," she said when he'd finished.

She was a slim, pretty woman who wore her graying hair cut short. She worked in an insurance office in town and she still had on the skirt and blouse she'd worn to work that day. She'd kicked off her shoes, however.

"It looks like murder," Rhodes said. "I don't see how it could be anything else."

"And someone tried to run you down with a monster truck while you were looking at a moonshine still."

"It wasn't a monster. Just a pickup. It wasn't as bad as I made it sound."

Ivy said, "Ha!"

"I'm fine," Rhodes assured her. "Not a scratch on me. A quick bath and I'll be clean as a whistle."

"Did you say clean as a weasel?"

"That, too."

They were in the kitchen, and Sam, the coal black cat, was rubbing against the leg of the chair where Rhodes sat while scratching the top of Sam's head.

Rhodes sneezed a couple of times. Ivy had told him that he wasn't really allergic to Sam, that his sneezing was some kind of psychological reaction. Rhodes couldn't see that it made any difference. A sneeze was a sneeze.

Yancey, the Pomeranian, watched from the doorway. He didn't like Sam in the least. For his part, Sam hardly deigned to notice the dog.

"I'd better take Yancey outside for a few minutes and let him play with Speedo," Rhodes said. "He needs a little exercise to work off his hostility toward the cat."

"Do it before you bathe," Ivy said.

Rhodes called Yancey, who crossed the room warily, keeping a close eye on Sam all the way. Sam ignored him and went over to the refrigerator to lie down, so that the warm air venting from beneath it would blow on him.

Once the cat was out of his way, Yancey became more animated, yapping eagerly for Rhodes to open the door and let him outside.

Rhodes pushed the screen door open and Yancey bounded out. Speedo, the Border collie who lived outside and had his own Styrofoam igloo to stay in, barked a greeting.

While the two dogs, big and little, chased each other around the backyard, Rhodes sat on the steps. It wasn't much cooler now that night had fallen than it had been during the day. Rhodes hoped it would cool off before morning. Then his thoughts turned to Terry Crawford's death.

Rhodes didn't think there was anything to Judge Parry's theory about vigilantes. Anyone who'd gone to the mobile home looking for a meth lab wouldn't have found one, and it was unlikely that anyone would have found the still. Besides, Rhodes just didn't believe any of the academy members would have taken such a drastic step.

The explosion could have been an accident, and most likely was, but it certainly hadn't killed Terry. So the big questions were who'd been with him, and why he had been shot. Rhodes also wanted to know how Terry had gotten out of the house, and why he'd left it. Not to mention how he'd ended up down the hill near the creek.

Added to those questions were a few that Rhodes had about the truck. Who'd been driving it, and why had he been there? Was there some connection to the academy class?

Max Schwartz and Jackee had a good reason to be angry with Terry, as Rhodes had seen that afternoon. Had their anger led to something more?

As usual, Rhodes knew that he'd have even more questions once he started digging into Terry's life. It might not be like chasing a serial killer, but it would no doubt cause quite a stir in Blacklin County before it was all over.

Rhodes stood up and got the Ol' Roy sack from the back porch to feed Speedo. While the dog was eating, Rhodes put fresh water in his bowl as Yancey yapped and danced around him.

When Speedo came over and lapped the water, Rhodes went back inside for his bath. Yancey followed him, keeping a watchful eye out for the cat.

TEN

Supper that evening was to be eggplant Parmesan, one of the new recipes that Ivy was trying out. She told Rhodes that eggplant had very few calories, was high in fiber, and was delicious when spiced up a little.

"I can grill it instead of frying it," she said. "That way, there's no fat from the oils."

Rhodes kind of missed fat, to tell the truth, though he didn't see any need to mention that. He asked Ivy what she knew about the Crawfords.

"Not much. I would never have guessed that they were making whiskey."

"I wonder where they were selling it," Rhodes said.

"I've been thinking about that while you were in the yard. I heard that you could buy whiskey at Dooley's."

Dooley's was a roadhouse that had opened just outside of town, down the highway from the community college. The owner, Jerry Kergan, had owned a little diner in Thurston, a small town in the southern part of the county. The diner hadn't done too well, mainly because Thurston was too small to support it, and Kergan had told people that he thought a new location was what he needed to make a success of things, a place where there were more people. So he'd moved to Clearview, bought an old building, and converted it into a restaurant with a bar and a dance floor.

The bar served only beer, and the dance floor didn't get much use except on Saturday nights, when Kergan brought in a live band to perform.

Or the bar was *supposed* to serve only beer. Rhodes told Ivy that he hadn't heard the rumor about the whiskey.

"You should have mentioned it," he said.

"It was just something I heard in passing at the office," she said. "I didn't ever think of it again. I didn't believe it, and I just put it out of my mind."

Rhodes looked over at Sam. The cat was watching him with its yellow eyes, its tail moving slowly back and forth. Yancey was nowhere to be seen. He was probably in another room, wishing the cat would disappear—permanently.

Rhodes stifled a sneeze.

"It makes sense that the Crawfords were selling whiskey in big amounts," he said. "They'd have to if they wanted to make any money. Just having people drive up and buy a bottle wouldn't be profitable enough."

"I'd have told you about Dooley's if I'd thought it was important," Ivy said.

"I know you would. I wonder if anywhere else in town is selling whiskey."

"I didn't say that Mr. Kergan was. I just mentioned a rumor."

"It's something I'll have to check out. If you hear any more rumors, let me know."

"I will. Shall I start grilling the eggplant?"

Rhodes noticed that she hadn't changed clothes. He wasn't any Sage Barton when it came to women, but he could take a hint. He said, "Why don't we eat out tonight."

"Good idea," Ivy said. "I wonder why I didn't think of it. I'll put on my shoes. Where do you want to go?"

"I was thinking about Dooley's," Rhodes said.

IT WAS NEARLY NINE O'CLOCK when they got started toward the roadhouse. They went in Rhodes's old Edsel, a car he drove only often enough to keep the battery charged. It's fish-mouthed body style always attracted attention when he got it out of the garage.

"Do you think you'll be getting into any gunfights tonight?" Ivy said as they drove along.

"You've been thinking about Claudia and Jan's book," Rhodes said.

Like him, she'd read the manuscript. She'd told Rhodes that she thought it would sell very well.

"I don't think I'll be able to go to the signing tomorrow," Rhodes said. "I'll be working on the Crawford murder."

"You have to go. This is a big deal for Jan and Claudia. It's their launch party."

The women had explained to Rhodes that because they both had full-time jobs, they couldn't take time to go on a real tour across the country like the big-name writers did, but they planned to sign in as many places as they could on weekends. They hoped to cover most of Texas and maybe even get into Oklahoma.

"If the book does well, they might get a real tour next time," Ivy said. "Maybe they can even quit their jobs and write full-time."

"How often does that happen?" Rhodes said.

"According to Claudia, not often enough."

That pretty much confirmed Rhodes's suspicions.

As they passed through the downtown area, or what was left of it, Ivy said, "Randy Lawless does all right for himself, doesn't he?"

They were at the stop sign where one of the town's two red lights had once been. There wasn't any need for lights now. Most of the traffic had followed Wal-Mart out to the east side of town.

Across the street, where an entire city block of buildings had fallen down or been demolished, sat the immaculate new law offices of Randall Lawless & Associates. It was a big white building, and while it didn't occupy the entire block, it sat in the middle of it and took up plenty of room. The rest of the block was a parking lot, except for a small rock garden. People around Clearview had taken to calling the new building "the Lawj Mahal."

"I have a feeling a lawyer like Lawless makes more money than the sheriff," Rhodes said.

"I didn't marry you for your money," Ivy told him.

"Why did you, then?"

"Because you're clean." Ivy slid across the wide seat to get close to him. "As a weasel."

"I knew you had a good reason," Rhodes said.

THE BUILDING THAT HOUSED Dooley's had once been a restaurant that was part of a national chain. For some reason, people in Clearview hadn't liked the food, or had preferred the local restaurants like the Jolly Tamale and the RoundUp. Dooley's, however, seemed to be doing all right. There were ten or twelve cars in the asphalt parking lot, which Rhodes thought was a good number for that time of night. Even on Friday, people in Clearview ate early and went home. If some of them were still around after that, Dooley's must have something to attract them. One of the cars was a red Chrysler convertible, and Rhodes wondered what Max Schwartz was doing there.

When he got out of the Edsel, Rhodes found out what the attraction was. A sandwich-board sign stood by the front door of the restaurant. It said LIVE MUSIC TONIGHT. ORIGINAL SONGS BY C. P. BENTON.

"Wasn't he in your academy?" Ivy asked.

"He was, but that's not where he learned to play the guitar."

"I didn't think it was. I wonder what his original songs are like."

"We're about to find out," Rhodes said.

He pulled open the door and they went inside. A podium stood nearby, and a man behind it asked them if they'd like to eat or go to the bar.

The man was stout, with a round face and graying hair parted in the middle. Rhodes had never met Jerry Kergan, but he assumed this must be the owner.

"Are you Mr. Kergan?" he said.

The man nodded. "That's me. And you are?"

"Dan Rhodes. This is my wife, Ivy."

"You're the sheriff," Kergan said, showing no signs of worry or dread. "It's a pleasure to have you here."

"Thanks," Rhodes said. "We'd like to eat. Maybe we'll visit the bar later."

Kergan didn't have any objections. He took a couple of menus from a stack on a stand beside him.

"Would you like to be seated near the entertainer?" he asked.

"Sounds good," Rhodes told him, and Kergan led them into the dining area, a large open room with well-spaced tables around the hardwood dance floor.

C. P. Benton sat on a stool on a small elevated stage near the back wall. He wore his hat, of course, along with black pants and a T-shirt that said I ♥ MATH. He didn't really have the build to wear a T-shirt, in Rhodes's opinion, but then neither did Rhodes.

A microphone stand and mike stood in front of Benton. He was tuning his guitar, paying no attention to the diners, and he didn't see Rhodes.

Kergan led Rhodes and Ivy to a vacant table near the stage and put the menus on it. "Is this all right?"

"It's fine," Rhodes said.

Before he sat down, he looked around the room. Max Schwartz and his wife sat across the room. They were the only people in the room that Rhodes recognized. Schwartz raised his hand for an unenthusiastic wave.

Kergan pulled out a chair for Ivy. As she sat, he said, "Your waiter will be with you in a minute."

He walked away, and Ivy said, "He didn't seem intimidated by the handsome crime-busting sheriff."

"He just doesn't know how dangerous I am," Rhodes said.

Just as he finished speaking, C. P. Benton tapped on the mike and said, "Is this thing on?"

"It's on," someone yelled.

"Good. I'd like to begin my show by playing one of my own compositions and a favorite of mine. I call it 'It's Your Birthday, So Wear your Birthday Suit.'"

Ivy leaned toward Rhodes. "I'm not sure I want to hear this."

Rhodes wasn't sure, either, but the song turned out to be fairly amusing. Benton's voice was deep and not exactly suited to carrying the melody, but Rhodes didn't mind. Benton's playing wasn't on a professional level, either, any more than his singing was, but Rhodes didn't care about that, either.

After the song, Benton told a couple of jokes, or Rhodes figured that's what they were supposed to be. It seemed to him that it took Benton a lot longer than necessary to get them told. Then Benton launched into another song, this one entitled "The Enemy of My Enema is My Friend." Or Rhodes thought that was the title. He wasn't quite sure.

The server came and took their order. Rhodes went for the chicken-fried steak. He figured he might as well live dangerously, because he was sure to get the grilled eggplant sooner or later.

Ivy got soup and a salad, but even that didn't make Rhodes feel guilty. He looked around the restaurant. No one was drinking anything stronger than tea or coffee. There was no sign of anything like moonshine.

Ivy saw him studying the patrons. She said, "I think that

rumor was all wrong. I don't see any sign of hard liquor being served here."

Neither did Rhodes. It would have been a risky proposition so close to town, with someone almost sure to report any untoward incident. The college crowd might have been interested, but Dooley's didn't attract the college crowd. The students were all commuters who left the campus as soon as their classes were over. Some of them might have eaten at Dooley's at lunchtime, but not in the evenings.

He wondered, however, about Schwartz and Benton. Here they both were at Dooley's, and there was that rumor about the whiskey. Maybe there was some connection after all.

The server brought their food, and Rhodes ate his steak, enjoying the cream gravy and mashed potatoes that went with it. After the table had been cleared, the server asked if they wanted dessert. Rhodes thought about apple pie with cheese on top, or maybe vanilla ice cream, but he didn't want to push his luck, so he asked for the check.

Benton finished his short set to mild applause and set his guitar against the wall. He stepped down off the stage and walked over to Rhodes's table.

"Good evening, Sheriff," he said. "I thought I saw you out here. How did you like the songs?"

"A little odd for this town," Rhodes said. "But I liked them."

He introduced Ivy. By that time, they'd been joined by the Schwartzes, so Rhodes had to make further introductions.

Everyone found a chair, and soon they were all chatting like old friends. Rhodes asked Benton how it was that a college math teacher came to be singing in a roadhouse.

"I just do it for fun," Benton said. "I'm a versatile guy. Did you ever hear of Tom Lehrer? He taught math at Harvard, but he was famous for his satirical musical recordings."

Rhodes said he wasn't sure he'd ever heard of Lehrer.

"Well, that was a long time ago," Benton said. "I have a CD of his material, though."

"You'd be better off listening to the Kingston Trio," Schwartz said. "Now that's what I call music."

"I can do 'Scotch and Soda,'" Benton told him, and Schwartz recoiled in mock horror, his dark eyes large behind the lenses of his glasses.

"Don't," he said. "Just don't. No one should sing that except Bob Shane."

Benton looked hurt, as if he thought his voice was just as good as anybody's.

Jackee changed the subject. She said, "Have you caught Terry Crawford's killer?"

"No," Rhodes said, "but it's early yet. I have a few ideas."

"Anything you can share?"

"No, not now."

"Are we suspects?" Schwartz asked. "You can say so. It won't hurt our feelings."

"You're suspects," Rhodes said.

Schwartz looked crestfallen, as if his feelings were hurt.

"I'm sure you can account for your whereabouts this morning," Rhodes said to cheer him up. "So you have nothing to worry about."

Schwartz looked at Jackee, who looked at the floor.

"You *can* account for your whereabouts, can't you?" Rhodes said.

"Sure, sure," Schwartz said. "We were at the store. Isn't that right, Seepy?"

Seepy? Rhodes thought. Then he got it. *C. P.* had become *Seepy*.

Benton's eyes betrayed his confusion. "I'm sure you were," he said. "I have to go do my closing set now."

He stood up and went back to the stage.

"I hope he doesn't try to do any Kingston Trio songs," Schwartz said. "He'd screw them up."

"He didn't seem so sure you were at your store this morning," Rhodes said.

"We only asked him because we were there together," Jackee said. "Max and me, I mean."

"Yeah," Schwartz said. "We'd just be alibiing each other. Being a lawyer, I know how much you lawmen like that kind of thing."

"Better than no alibi at all," Rhodes said.

"It sure is. Well, I guess we'd better be going. Nice to see you, Sheriff. Nice to meet you, Ivy."

Schwartz and Jackee left, and Ivy said, "They're a nice couple."

"I don't trust them," Rhodes said, though it was hard to think of either of them as killers.

"What you mean is, you don't believe them. There's a difference."

"Not much of one," Rhodes said.

ELEVEN

RHODES LEFT IVY to listen to Seepy Benton.

"He can entertain you while I talk to Jerry Kergan."

"You're just trying to protect me in case Kergan pulls a gun on you."

Rhodes laughed. "Nobody's going to pull a gun on me. I'll be back in a few minutes."

He went into the foyer. Kergan wasn't at the podium. Instead, the server was standing there, looking bored. He was a young man, probably a student at the college, and Rhodes asked him where Kergan was.

"He went out back to smoke, just like every night."

The Clearview city council, in a controversial move, had voted to make all restaurants within the city limits comply with a nonsmoking policy. That didn't sit well with some of the owners, who claimed that it would cost them business, but everyone had eventually gone along with it.

"Through there," the young man said, pointing to the swinging doors that led to the kitchen.

Rhodes thanked him. He started to go through the doors, but he thought he should pay a visit to the bar first. Two men sat on stools, leaning forward, their elbows resting on the bar. Both of them had beers in front of them as they sat watching an Astros game on a flat-screen TV monitor that hung on the wall behind the bar. According to the box at the top of the screen, the game was in the ninth inning, and the Astros were behind by six runs. So what else was new?

The bartender looked at Rhodes, hopeful that he had another customer, but Rhodes just nodded and went back to the foyer, then over to the swinging doors.

He went through the kitchen, which smelled of both fried food and disinfectant. Rhodes was glad to see that the place appeared relatively clean. The county health inspector would be pleased, too.

He nodded to one of the cooks, who looked vaguely familiar, and went out through the back door. It was dark outside, the only light coming from a quarter moon and a light high on a pole at one end of the building. Rhodes could smell the garbage in the Dumpster.

Kergan stood about ten yards away, leaning back against the wall of the restaurant. Rhodes saw the tip of his cigarette glow red as he drew on it.

The night air was hot and dry, and there was no breeze. Rhodes thought he'd feel pretty much the same if he were to stand inside a furnace. He went over to join Kergan.

"Hello again, Sheriff," Kergan said. "Did you come out for a smoke?"

"I don't smoke," Rhodes said.

"I do." Kergan held up his right hand, the cigarette resting between his first two fingers. "I know they're bad for me, but I like the way they taste."

He took a deep drag and dropped the cigarette to the ground. He mashed it with the toe of his shoe, then picked up the dead butt, walked over to the Dumpster, and raised the lid. The smell of garbage became a little more obvious. He flipped the butt into the Dumpster and dropped the lid with a clang.

"If you didn't come out here to smoke," he said, "what did you come for?"

"Conversation," Rhodes said.

"Well, I'm not much of a talker unless you want to talk about my business. That's the only thing I know."

"That's good, since that's what I want to talk about."

"Then I'm your man. What do you want to ask me?"

"Tell me about your liquor license."

"What?"

Rhodes repeated what he'd said.

"I didn't think asking that question was in your job description. I'm right with the TABC, if that's what you're wondering about. My liquor license is displayed in the bar. You can take a look."

Kergan pulled a package of cigarettes from his shirt pocket and shook one out. He put the pack back, stuck the cigarette in his mouth, and lit it with a disposable lighter from a pants pocket. He blew out a plume of smoke and didn't seem inclined to say any more.

"I've heard rumors that you might be selling something other than beer in the bar," Rhodes said.

"Then the rumors are wrong."

"Most rumors are. I didn't see any sign that you were doing anything wrong."

"That's because I'm not." Kergan blew out smoke. "You're on the wrong track, Sheriff. I'm just a guy trying to get a restaurant business started."

"You seem to be doing all right."

"It's not as good as it looks. I have a lot of overhead. It's hard to get a start in this business."

Rhodes knew that. A number of restaurants had started and failed in Clearview over the years, and it was hard to figure why they hadn't done well while others had.

"Maybe the music will bring in the crowds," he said.

Kergan laughed. "You call that stuff Benton plays music? I just let Benton sing here because he begged me."

"He sounded all right to me."

"That shows what you know. Come back tomorrow night when the Ring-Tail Tooters are here. Now there's a band."

Rhodes had never heard of the Tooters. "Maybe I will," he said.

"You do that," Kergan said, dismissing Rhodes, who went back inside.

Ivy was at the table, laughing at some line in Benton's song, but nearly everyone else had left.

"Do you want to hear the rest?" Rhodes asked her.

"Not especially. Let's go home."

THE PARKING LOT was practically deserted, and Rhodes noticed that it wasn't much better lighted than the rear of the restaurant had been. While there wasn't a great deal of petty crime in Clear-view, it could be dangerous to park in the farthest corners of the lot if someone decided to try a car jacking or a purse snatching.

Rhodes opened the door of the Edsel for Ivy, then started around to the driver's side of the car. As he rounded the front of the car, he glanced at the highway and saw a pair of head-lights moving fast—too fast, far above the legal speed limit for that stretch of highway.

There wasn't much Rhodes could do about it. He wasn't going to get into a high-speed chase in an Edsel that was nearly fifty years old. He hoped one of the deputies on duty would spot the car and ticket the driver, maybe get him off the road.

The headlights slowed, and Rhodes thought the driver must have come to his senses. Then he realized that the driver was going to pull into the restaurant's parking lot.

Rhodes couldn't give him a ticket because had hadn't clocked his speed, but he could give him a little lecture. It probably wouldn't do any good, but it would make him feel better.

He waited beside his car, holding the door open, and the truck made a turn into the lot. Only when he saw the heavy brush guard did Rhodes realize that it was the same truck that had chased him earlier in the day.

The driver of the truck seemed to recognize him at just about the same time. He cut the wheels, and the truck swerved in Rhodes's direction, tires squealing on the asphalt.

The headlights of the oncoming truck shone in Rhodes's eyes, and he couldn't see who was behind the dark windshield, which was starred where the bullet from Rhodes's pistol had gone through it that afternoon.

This time, there was nowhere for Rhodes to run. The wall of the restaurant was behind him, and the car was on one side. If he moved to the other side, the truck would smash him up against the wall like a bug.

Rhodes jumped into the Edsel. He grabbed for the handle to pull the door shut behind him, but he missed.

At the last second the truck turned aside, as if the driver had decided he didn't want to crash into the wall. The back of the truck slammed into the Edsel's taillight, knocking the car a quarter turn to the right and throwing Rhodes hard against the steering wheel. Ivy had put on her seat belt already, so she didn't hit the dashboard.

Rhodes fumbled at his ankle holster. The Velco made a ripping sound, and he had the pistol in his hand.

"Are you all right?" he asked.

"I guess," Ivy replied.

She sounded breathless. Rhodes was breathless, too, and his chest hurt. He hoped it was just bruised and that he didn't have any cracked ribs. He stepped out of the car and hobbled off after the truck, which had scraped along the side of the building and turned the corner.

"Where are you going?" Ivy asked.

"After that truck," Rhodes told her, nearly tripping on the truck's rearview mirror, which was lying where it had fallen after being knocked off by the wall. He shoved the mirror aside and kept going, though it hurt to breathe.

He heard the howl of breaks behind the building, then a crash, followed by the grinding screech of steel on concrete. The truck's engine roared.

Rhodes got to the back of the restaurant, and, forgetting everything he'd ever learned, known, and experienced, made the turn around the corner without first having a look.

The truck was coming straight at him, its high beams blazing.

He could have planted his feet, stood his ground, and maybe gotten off one shot before the brush guard hit him. He had a flash of himself spread-eagled on the front of it like a character in a Bugs Bunny cartoon.

So he didn't take the time to shoot. He threw himself to the side, landing on his left shoulder. He rolled over a time or two and wound up on his back.

The big tires hissed by him on the asphalt. The truck squealed around the corner and was gone.

Rhodes lay on his back for a few seconds, making sure that he could still breathe. Now his shoulder hurt as much as his chest, but at least his lungs worked. That was bound to be a good sign.

He sat up and noticed that he was still holding his pistol. Another good sign. A lawman doesn't let go of his weapon.

"Can you stand up?" Ivy asked.

She stood in front of him, looking down. Rhodes hadn't noticed her arrival.

"I'm fine," he said, and with a little effort he got to his feet. He stuck the pistol in his pocket and tried to brush himself off.

"You don't look fine. What happened back here?"

Rhodes wasn't sure. He turned to see if Kergan was still around.

As he turned, the back door of the restaurant opened and people started to come out to see what all the commotion was about.

Someone screamed. Rhodes didn't know who it was. He walked to where the Dumpster sat. It had been shoved five or six feet from its original position. Big gouges in the asphalt showed its path.

Kergan was in front of the Dumpster, looking like something that belonged inside it. The truck had hit him, then pushed him against the Dumpster. Kergan had been squashed, but not like a cartoon character. Like a flesh and blood man. Mangled flesh and too much blood. Rhodes was glad for the bad lighting.

Rhodes told everyone to go back inside. Some of the more morbid among them wanted to get a better look at Kergan's remains, but Rhodes didn't allow it.

When they tried to push past him anyway, he told them to get back in or he'd arrest them. That did the trick. They left, although reluctantly. Rhodes knew they'd be talking about what they'd seen for weeks. It wasn't that they were bad people. It was just that violent death had a way of arousing a kind of curiosity in them that they might not even have known was there.

"What are you going to do?" Ivy asked. Her eyes looked stricken.

"Make some calls," Rhodes told her.

TWELVE

MUCH LATER, after the justice of the peace had declared Kergan dead, after the ambulance had taken him away, after the scene had been secured as well as possible, Rhodes walked back around to the front of the restaurant, where Ivy was waiting for him in the Edsel.

Seepy Benton stood beside the car, talking to Ivy. When he saw Rhodes approaching, he said something to Ivy and went to meet Rhodes.

"I've been talking to your wife," he said.

"We trained lawmen tend to notice that kind of thing."

"I liked talking to her. She's very nice."

"I've noticed that, too."

"I don't blame you for being a little surly. It must be hard to have to deal with dead bodies and murder."

Rhodes didn't think he was being surly. He was tired and his chest hurt, but he wasn't surly.

"Were you too squeamish to come out back and have a look?" he said.

"I don't like to look at things like that. I'm not squeamish. I'd just rather not."

Rhodes didn't blame him.

"You probably didn't hang around out here just to talk to my nice wife," Rhodes said.

"No, but I had a good reason. I don't know if you're aware of it, but I was quite a help to the police in the town I used to live in."

"I believe you mentioned that a time or two in the academy classes," Rhodes said.

"I did? I don't remember."

Rhodes just waited.

"What I was thinking," Benton said, "was that I might be able to help you out with this murder."

"It might have been just an accident," Rhodes said. "The driver was lost, and Kergan got between the truck and the Dumpster."

"That's what I'd say if I were the driver and I got caught, but I don't believe it. I'll bet you don't believe it, either."

"No," Rhodes said. "I don't believe it."

"And even if it was an accident, it was a hit-and-run. That's not murder, but it's not good."

"No, it's not good."

"So I was right. I'm right about being able to help you with this, too."

"I don't think that would be a good idea," Rhodes told him.

"That's because you don't know the whole story. I have some information that you don't have."

It had been a long day, and Rhodes was tired. He didn't feel like dragging information out of Benton the way he had to drag it out of Hack and Lawton.

"Tell me what it is," he said.

"One of the things we learned in the academy is that one part of an investigation is learning about the victim's associates."

"I'm the sheriff," Rhodes said. "Remember?"

"So you'd know all that, I guess. I teach math, and sometimes I tend to forget what people know."

Next, Rhodes thought, I'll be getting a lecture on the importance of fractions.

"You know that Mr. Kergan's wife is dead?" Benton said.

Rhodes had heard that. "I know. You mentioned something about associates."

"That's right, I did. I've been singing here for the last three Fridays, and I've seen some of the people who come and go. Some of them don't even eat here. They just go into Mr. Kergan's office, along with Mr. Kergan. After awhile, they come back out and leave."

"What people?"

"I didn't know all of them, but I knew two of them."

"And sooner or later you're probably even going to tell me who they are."

Benton gave a rueful grin. "I do tend to take my time about telling things. It's one of my little failings, not that I have many of them. My students mention that one on the evaluations now and then."

Rhodes wondered what it would take to move Benton along to the point. Something must have shown in his face, because Benton held up his hand as if to ward off a blow.

"The Crawfords," Benton said. "That's who I was talking about. Larry and Terry Crawford. They'd come into the restaurant, and Mr. Kergan would take them to his office. They'd leave later without eating. So obviously they weren't here for the food."

"Obviously," Rhodes said.

"I'll tell you who else was here, too. You know the commissioners?"

"I'm the sheriff, remember?"

"Maybe it's because I'm a teacher, but I tend to overexplain things, even when it's not necessary. Of course you know the commissioners. There's one of them who doesn't like me much. He thinks I'm a pest."

"Imagine that," Rhodes said.

Benton looked at Rhodes and shook his head. "I'm not a pest. I just want people to do their jobs and mow the ditches now and then."

"Right," Rhodes said. "What do the ditches have to do with this?"

"One of the people who spends time in Mr. Kergan's office is the commissioner for my district."

"Mikey Burns."

"That's the one," Benton said.

Benton was right about having some interesting information, Rhodes thought. He considered apologizing but decided not to. It might give Benton the idea he was being more helpful than he actually was.

"And there's a woman, too," Benton continued. "I don't know her name, but I know she works with computers. She's been out at the college a time or two, talking to some of the IT people."

"What's she look like?"

"She's short, and she has blond hair. Not old. Not young. Kind of cute."

"Mel Muller," Rhodes said, though he wasn't sure.

Benton shook his head. "I don't know."

"Don't worry," Rhodes said. "I'll find out."

RHODES SENT BENTON AWAY, then told Ivy to take the Edsel home and go to bed.

"How will you get home?"

"Duke will take me."

Duke Pearson was the deputy who'd responded to one of the calls Rhodes had made.

"Are you all right?" Ivy asked.

"Just bruised."

"And not as clean as a weasel, either."

"It's a hazardous job."

"But somebody has to do it."

"Right. I'll try not to wake you up when I get in."

"You'd better wake me. I want to know you're home."

Rhodes promised he'd wake her if that was what she wanted, and Ivy drove away.

Rhodes went inside the restaurant to make sure that Kergan's office was sealed. It was.

Duke Pearson was just about finished with his questioning of the employees. The server whom Rhodes had talked to earlier was waiting his turn in the foyer, while Duke was talking to one of the cooks in the big dining room. Rhodes called the server over and asked his name.

"Ralph Meadows. Everybody calls me Scooter."

Scooter was about twenty, Rhodes guessed. He had brown hair that was cut very short, a wide face with a big nose, and ears that stuck out a little too much. He still looked a little shocked at what had happened.

"All right, Scooter," Rhodes said. "How long have you been working here?"

"Ever since the place opened. I live in Thurston, and Mr. Kergan knows my daddy. Knew him, I guess I should say. I still can't believe he's dead."

"Your father's Henry Meadows?"

"That's right. You know him?"

Scooter seemed surprised that anyone would know his father, but Rhodes had met the man a couple of times. He was the only thing resembling a mechanic in Thurston and did minor car repairs in the shell of an old building that had once housed a service station. There was no service station in Thurston now, just a couple of gas pumps at a little convenience store out on the main highway that bypassed the town.

"Not well. He got you this job?"

"Yeah. He talked to Mr. Kergan about it. I guess I don't have a job now, though."

Rhodes didn't know what would happen to the restaurant.

Kergan wasn't married, and Rhodes didn't know about the next of kin.

"Has anybody told Miss Muller?" Scooter asked.

"Melanie Muller?" Rhodes said.

He'd told Benton he'd find out, but he hadn't known it would be quite so easy.

"I think that's her name. She does computer stuff. I think she and Mr. Kergan were pretty good friends."

"You mean they were dating?"

"Do old people date?"

Kergan was around fifty. Rhodes figured that to Scooter that was about the same as being around a hundred.

"Sometimes they do," Rhodes said. "Just for company. Somebody to watch TV with. You know."

"I guess," Scooter said. He looked doubtful. "Anyway, Miss Muller was here a lot, and she ate for free."

"Did she spend any time in Kergan's office with him?"

"She went in there sometimes. They closed the door."

Rhodes asked a few more questions, the standard ones about enemies or people that Kergan might have had trouble with in the restaurant, but Scooter was no help. He didn't know a thing about Larry and Terry, though he thought "two guys who looked alike" had been in several times to talk to Kergan.

"Do you think I should come to work tomorrow?" Scooter asked when the interview was over.

"I don't think you need to bother," Rhodes told him.

DUKE PEARSON DROVE Rhodes home when the interviews were completed. He'd been with the department for only a few months. For years, he'd worked as a deputy in a small county in West Texas, but his wife was from Clearview, and they'd moved there to take care of her mother, who was in the first stages of Alzheimer's.

Pearson was a burly man with graying hair that he combed back on the sides. He smiled a lot, and people seemed to like him. He was also good at his job, and Rhodes was glad to have him in the department. Unfortunately, he hadn't found out much from the people he'd interviewed, not even as much as Rhodes had found out from Scooter.

"I got the feeling they didn't want to talk about their boss even if he was dead," Pearson said. His voice was gravelly. "I don't know if that means anything."

Rhodes didn't know for sure, either, but he thought it might.

"Something was going on at the restaurant," Rhodes said. "I don't know what it was—yet."

He brought Pearson up to date on the Crawfords.

"So you don't think Kergan's death was an accident?" Pearson said.

"Let's say it's highly unlikely."

"And you think the Crawfords are tied into it?"

"If I were a betting man, which I'm not, I'd lay good odds that they were."

"Anything you want me to be looking for tonight?"

"That truck," Rhodes said. He described it again. "If you see it, call it in. Follow it if you can. Don't try to stop it."

"After seeing what happened to Kergan, I'm not likely to stand in front of it, if that's what you mean."

"That's what I mean," Rhodes said.

IT WAS LATE when Rhodes got home, well after midnight. Speedo wanted to play, but Rhodes wasn't up to it. His chest hurt, and he wanted to take a bath and go to bed. He found Speedo's ball and threw it for the dog to fetch a couple of times, but that was all the fun he could stand.

"Sorry, Speedo," he said. "Maybe in the morning."

Speedo stood and watched him as he went in through the

back door, but when Rhodes looked back outside, the collie was already in his igloo.

Sam was still in the kitchen, sleeping on the floor near the refrigerator. Yancey was nowhere to be seen.

Rhodes went into the bathroom and took off his shirt. A big area in the middle of his chest had turned an ugly yellowish color, and it was starting to turn purple in places. It would be even more colorful in the next day or so.

While he showered, Rhodes thought about everything that had happened that day. There was a lot to think about, and he wondered just how Mikey Burns and Melanie Muller fit into the puzzle whose pieces he was pushing around. And Kergan. What the heck was going on at Dooley's? What did the Crawfords have to do with it?

Rhodes's brain wasn't functioning at peak efficiency, and he kept thinking there was something he'd seen that day that was out of place, a puzzle piece that might fit if he could only figure out what it was.

But he couldn't. It was too late, and he was too tired. He dried off and got in bed beside Ivy.

"Were you planning to wake me up?" she said as he lay down.

"I was going to wait till you started snoring. Then I was going to prod you a little."

"I don't snore," Ivy said.

"Only in a very genteel way."

"I'm going to prod you if you say that again."

"I think I'll just go to sleep," Rhodes said.

"I'm glad you're home."

"Me, too," Rhodes said.

THIRTEEN

THE NEXT MORNING began well. Rhodes's shoulder and chest didn't hurt as much as he'd thought they would, and he figured they'd be fine in another day or so. He went into the backyard and played with Speedo and Yancey, who took turns chasing the ball and bringing it back to him. They never really wanted to let him take it from them, and part of the game was to let them growl and shake their heads when he tried to remove it.

It was already getting warm, so Rhodes didn't lark around with the dogs for long. He let Yancey back into the house and drove to the jail.

The day started to go downhill when he arrived there. Hack extracted all the details about the previous night's events at Dooley's from Rhodes while he was writing up his report and then informed him that Ruth hadn't found any prints on the whiskey jars.

"They must've wiped 'em, or used gloves," Hack said.

Rhodes wasn't surprised. Crawford wasn't entirely stupid.

But that wasn't all. Hack also told Rhodes, after a bit of coaxing, that there'd already been several calls that morning, one of which concerned an infestation of possums in Mrs. Hallie Owens's attic.

"Been chewin' on the wires up there," Hack said. "Miz Owens is afraid they might cause a fire. You're supposed to go there and evict 'em."

"Why me?" Rhodes said.

He took off the reading glasses he'd had to put on to do the report and stuck them back in his shirt pocket.

"Because you're the high sheriff," Lawton said. "It's your job."

"That's right," Hack agreed. "Miz Owens asked for you in person because she voted for you in the last election, and she figures you owe her."

"Send Buddy," Rhodes said.

"He's at the courthouse checkin' on Jamey Hamilton's car registration. After that, he's got to call those Dodge dealers and talk to some welders. He's already checked the reports on stolen vehicles. Nothing about any old truck in them. Anyway, he won't have time to climb up in any attics."

"Have you heard from Ruth?"

"She'll be doin' her patrol, but her wrist is still hurtin'. No use for you to try sendin' her. She couldn't do the climbin'."

Rhodes wasn't going to do any climbing, either, not if he could help it. His chest was too sore.

"Call Mrs. Owens and tell her we'll send somebody out there later. Buddy's bound to finish with that other stuff pretty soon."

"Miz Owens is gonna be mighty disappointed when you don't show up," Hack said. "She asked for you specially."

"But if you don't go by her place, maybe you can handle the loose donkey," Lawton said, and Hack gave him a hostile stare.

"What loose donkey?" Rhodes said.

"The one at the car wash," Hack said, taking over. "I don't know if somebody was washin' it or not, so don't ask me that. All I know is we got a call, and there's a loose donkey at the car wash."

"Could be a mule," Lawton said. "Lots of people can't tell the difference."

"Donkeys're colored different, usually," Hack said. "Sound different for sure."

Rhodes wasn't interested in a lesson in donkey and mule identification.

"What this county needs is an animal-control officer," he said.

"Commissioners won't go for it. You've been doin' too good a job."

Rhodes knew Hack was right. He said, "Call Franklin Anderson about the donkey."

Anderson was a cowboy for hire. He worked on several ranches around the area, and he occasionally did jobs for the sheriff's department.

"He'll want to know who's gonna pay him."

"The owner will."

"And if we can't find the owner?"

"The county will."

The county had a fund for that kind of thing, but it wasn't a lot of money. The commissioners preferred it when the owner could be found and made to pay Anderson's fee.

"Maybe you could adopt it," Hack said. "You got a way of pickin' up animals on the job."

"Two dogs and a cat are more than enough. I don't think Speedo would like sharing the backyard with a donkey."

"Or a mule," Lawton said. "Dependin' on which one it is."

"Caller said a donkey," Hack reminded him. "I'm bettin' it's a donkey."

"Could be a burro," Lawton said. "Now, your burro really does look like a donkey."

"I thought a burro and a donkey were the same thing."

"See, that's where you're wrong. Your burro—"

"That's enough of that," Rhodes said.

Hack and Lawton looked at each other and stifled grins. Rhodes asked them if there were any other calls he needed to deal with.

"Nothin' important," Hack said. "But don't forget about Miz Owens's possums."

"Dogs might like a possum around the house," Lawton said. "I know a guy kept one for a pet once. He says—"

"Never mind," Rhodes told him.

The door of the jail opened and Jennifer Loam came in.

"Never mind what?" she said.

"Possums," Hack told her. "It's a big story. Front-page stuff. They're runnin' wild in Miz Hallie Owens's attic."

Jennifer didn't appear to be ready to yell "Stop the presses." "What I want to know about is Jerry Kergan."

Rhodes told her the bare facts, while trying not to appear too evasive.

"You don't have an identification on the truck?" she asked when he was finished.

Rhodes told her that Buddy was working on it. He didn't mention his other encounter with the truck or anything else that had happened at the Crawford place. Jennifer would make the connection soon enough, he figured.

"You have a big event scheduled this afternoon, don't you?" she said.

Rhodes had completely forgotten about the book signing, and he was sorry to be reminded.

"I'm not sure I can make it," he said.

"You better be there," Hack said. "You're gonna be famous, and you don't want to miss out on the beginnin'."

"I'll be covering it for the paper," Jennifer said. "I'll want some pictures of you and the authors. I think there'll be a big crowd."

Rhodes hoped no one would show up. "I'll be there if I can. I have a murder investigation going on."

"The signing won't take much of your time," Jennifer said. "I'll see you there."

"Don't count on me."

"All right, I won't, but I'm sure the authors will."

Jennifer left to drive to Dooley's for a picture of the Dumpster, and Rhodes told Hack that he was going over to the courthouse, where he had an office.

"You might check on Buddy while you're there," Hack said. "Unless he's left already."

Rhodes said that he would.

"What about them possums? Miz Owens is gonna call back sure as you're livin'."

"Tell her we're working on it," Rhodes said.

RHODES HAD ALWAYS LIKED his office in the courthouse for a couple of reasons. For one thing, it was private. He didn't have to listen to anybody discussing the difference between burros and donkeys.

Unfortunately, the other reason had recently been taken away from him. In the past, he'd been able to get Dr Pepper in glass bottles in the soft-drink machine near his office. Not anymore. The machine had been removed and replaced with an up-to-date model that dispensed plastic bottles. The only thing that surprised Rhodes was that the old machine hadn't been removed long before.

The good news, however, was that sometime within the past week, the Dr Peppers placed in the new machine all had little notices on the bottles declaring that the drinks were made with real sugar instead of corn syrup. For years, the only way Rhodes had been able to get Dr Pepper made with real sugar was to order it from the plant in Dublin, Texas, but now it seemed that other places were using real sugar again.

So while Rhodes had to suffer the plastic bottles, he got real sugar in his drink. And the drinks were in much bigger bottles. He still preferred the glass ones, but he figured that the real sugar was worth making a sacrifice for.

But there was another problem. The machine was so complicated that it often shook the Dr Pepper up and caused it to spew if Rhodes opened it as soon as he got it. He had to be careful.

He put his money in the machine, got the Dr Pepper, and went to his office. He left the drink on his desk without screwing off the cap and went down to the basement, where the tax office and vehicle-registration department were located. One of the clerks told him that Buddy was still there, and he asked her to send him up when he got through with what he was doing. The clerk said she'd be glad to do that, and Rhodes went back to his office. He took the stairs instead of the creaky elevator. That way, he got a little exercise and didn't have to worry about being trapped between floors.

The Dr Pepper was all right when Rhodes returned, so he opened it and took a swallow. It wasn't as cold as it would have been from a glass bottle, or so he thought, but it made him feel a little better, and he set the bottle down so that he could make a call to the TABC and let them know about the still he'd found at the Crawfords'.

The call didn't take long, though the man Rhodes talked to was surprised to hear what Rhodes had found.

"We don't get reports of more than one or two of those a year," he said. "You're sure about this?"

Rhodes wanted to say that he knew the difference between a still and a burro, but he didn't think the man would get the joke.

"I'm sure. It's a still all right. I'm trying to find the man who owns it."

He went on to explain the circumstances and said he'd let the TABC representative onto the property when he showed up. After he hung up, he had time to take another swallow of the Dr Pepper before Buddy came in.

Buddy had been with the sheriff's department almost as long as Rhodes had. He was whip-thin and had a low tolerance for wrongdoers. In the Old West, he'd have been a hanging judge.

Rhodes asked what he'd found out about the truck.

"Not a thing," Buddy said, sitting down in the chair across from Rhodes's desk. "That truck's not registered to Jamey Hamilton, at least not in this county. He drives a little Chevy S-Ten. I called the Dodge dealers in the counties around here, and they don't remember that bumper guard, so nobody installed it at a dealership. Or if it was, it was too long ago for anybody to remember it. I'll check the welders after I leave here, but I figure it was put on in some other county, too."

"Never mind about the welders," Rhodes said. "See what you can find out about Jamey Hamilton. I know he's lived in Obert for three or four years, but find out where he came from and what he did there."

"All right. I guess I can do that."

"I'm sure you can," Rhodes told him.

AFTER BUDDY LEFT, Rhodes finished his Dr Pepper and considered his next move. He couldn't decide whether to talk to Mikey Burns or Mel Muller first. He'd look for Crawford and Hamilton, but he didn't know where to start, and Ruth was looking for them anyway. Rhodes suspected that Lawless might know where they were. He'd talk to Lawless later.

He had an Indian Head penny in the center drawer of his desk. His father had given it to him when Rhodes was about to start the first grade. It was supposed to be his lucky piece. Rhodes didn't know if it had been lucky or not, but he'd managed to survive first grade and the rest of his education unscathed. Why, he'd even learned a couple of lines of poetry.

He opened the drawer and took out the penny. He'd carried it with him for so many years that the date on the coin was too rubbed to read, but he remembered that it had been 1902.

"Heads, Muller," he said. "Tails, Burns."

He flipped the coin. It spun in the air and landed on the desk.

Rhodes thought it might roll off, but it didn't. The Indian Head was showing.

"Mel Muller it is," he said.

He started to put the penny back into the drawer, but he slipped it in his pocket instead. He had a feeling he was going to need all the luck he could get.

FOURTEEN

MEL MULLER WASN'T any happier to see Rhodes than she'd been the day before, less so if anything. Her hair wasn't combed and her eyes were red. She held a tissue clenched in her hand.

"What do you want?" she said to Rhodes as he stood in the doorway of the manufactured home. "If it's about that Web site, you tell Mikey Burns to give me a call and I'll tell him what he can do with his damn Web site."

"It's not about the Web site," Rhodes said. "It's about Jerry Kergan."

Mel choked back a sob and opened the door wider. Rhodes went inside. The place didn't look any different. Somewhere a radio was playing songs from the 1950s. Rhodes recognized "Witch Doctor."

"I listen to the radio on the Internet," Mel said when he gave her an inquiring look. She brushed at her eyes with the tissue. "I hate listening to commercials."

"But 'Witch Doctor'?"

"I don't much like any of the music I grew up with. I mean, disco? Give me a break. Anyway, you didn't come here to discuss my taste in music."

"Can we sit down?" Rhodes asked.

Mel walked over to the easy chair and brushed the computer magazines off it and onto the floor.

"Have a seat," she said.

Rhodes sat in the chair, and Mel sat on the couch. She looked at Rhodes, waiting to hear what he had to say. The radio played "Tom Dooley." Hearing the voices of the Kingston Trio, Rhodes was reminded of Max Schwartz.

"You've heard about Jerry Kergan, I guess," Rhodes said.

Mel brushed at her eyes again. "I've heard. What do you care?"

"His death wasn't an accident. I'm going to find out who killed him and why."

"And you think I can help you?"

Her eyes were dry now, and hard. Rhodes didn't think she was going to cooperate.

"That's what I think," he said.

"Well, I can't help, no matter what you think. I would if I could, but I don't know a thing about what happened or why it happened or anything else. If you'll leave now, I'll get to work on that Web site you're so worried about."

"I'm not worried about it. Mikey Burns is. Which reminds me. I've been thinking about something you said last night."

Mel didn't appear to care what Rhodes remembered. She just looked at him.

"You said something to the effect that Mikey Burns wouldn't know a date if it bit him in the butt. I didn't think anything of it at the time, but now I wonder if you didn't mean a different kind of date from the one I had in mind."

Mel looked away. "I don't have any idea what you're talking about."

"I'll tell you, then. When I suggested that Burns talk to you about the Web site, he didn't want to have a thing to do with it. He insisted that I had to do it. I thought he might just be intimidated by you, but politicians don't intimidate that easily. It had to be something else."

"So?" Mel said. She wasn't going to make it easy.

"So I have a feeling you and Burns are better acquainted than I thought you were. You and Kergan knew each other pretty well, too. I'd like to know what was going on with the three of you."

The tissue Mel held had been wadded into a small, tight ball. She unwadded it and blew her nose. She got up and walked into the computer room, where she threw the tissue into a wastebasket.

Rhodes listened to Dicky Doo and the Don'ts sing "Click Clack" until she came back.

She sat back on the couch and said, "All right, what do you want me to say?"

"I want to hear about you and Burns, and I want you to tell me how Kergan comes into whatever relationship you had."

"I didn't have anything to do with running Jerry down."

"I didn't say you did."

"I don't think Mikey did, either."

Rhodes wasn't a hundred percent sure of that. He kept thinking about that black truck. It could have been one that was kept off the roads as a farm vehicle, as he'd first thought, but another place where a truck like that would go unremarked was a precinct barn like the one where Burns had his office.

"If you'll just tell me what was going on with the three of you," Rhodes said, "I might be able to make up my mind about what you and Burns might have done. Or not done."

"All right," Mel said. "I'll tell you. It's not very interesting, though. Excuse me."

She got up and left the room. Rhodes listened to someone singing about a little white cloud that cried. He couldn't remember the singer's name. When Mel returned, she held a box of tissues.

"In case I need one," she explained, setting the box on the coffee table before she sat on the couch.

"Like the little white cloud," Rhodes said.

She gave him a blank look.

"On the radio," Rhodes said. "Or the Internet. It was in a song that was playing."

"Oh."

"Right. Now about Mikey Burns."

"He and I have known each other for a while," Mel said. "When his wife died, he got interested in computers. Then when YTwoK was coming up, he got worried about what was going to happen. You remember YTwoK, don't you?"

"Well enough," Rhodes said.

He remembered that there had been some kind of worldwide near panic that computers everywhere would crash, throwing the cities and countries everywhere into crisis. Some people in Clearview had stockpiled food, even gone so far as to bury huge supplies of it in the country around town in preparation for the collapse of civilization.

It hadn't happened. Midnight came and went all over the world, and the computers kept right on computing, or whatever they did. Rhodes figured some residents of the county were still digging up food supplies.

He didn't see what any of this had to do with Mikey Burns, however.

"He hired me to check all his computers," Mel said. "He didn't want anything to happen to them. We got to know each other a little. One thing led to another. You know how it is, I'm sure."

Rhodes nodded. He didn't exactly know how it was, not being as steamy as Sage Barton, but he had a pretty good idea.

"We went out a few times. We got along. I thought he liked me more than he did, maybe. Anyway, it didn't last. He dropped me."

That would have been about the time Burns was running for commissioner, Rhodes thought.

"He didn't think I was the right kind of person to have around him when he was politicking," Mel said, confirming Rhodes's suspicions. "As soon as he got elected, he started to come around again. Fool that I was, I went out with him. Just when I thought things were getting serious, he dropped me again."

She reached for a tissue, pulled it out of the box, and crumpled it in her hand.

"I didn't go out with anyone for a while," she continued. "Then Jerry Kergan started looking around for a property where he could open a restaurant. Naturally, he needed somebody to install his computer system, and he thought a local person would be best."

"You, for instance," Rhodes said.

"Yes, me. He hired me, and after he renovated the building, I went to work for him. We got to be friends."

It seemed to Rhodes that she got to be friends with a lot of her clients, but so far she'd only mentioned two. He decided that he was too judgmental.

"I don't see how all this fits together," he said.

"It's like this. As soon as I started seeing Jerry, Mikey got interested again. Some men are like that."

Rhodes wouldn't know. He didn't think he was like that.

"Burns didn't like it that you were dating Kergan?"

"That's right, but it was too late. I wasn't going back to Mikey, not after the way he'd treated me. He talked to Jerry about it. Jerry just laughed at him. That's it. That's all there was to it."

"Why did Burns hire you to do the Web site for my department, then?"

"Oh, that was his way of trying to bribe me. Or maybe he hired me because he knows I'm good at what I do. That might be out of character for him, but it could happen. Anyway, he never threatened me or Jerry. It was no big deal."

Rhodes wondered if that was really all there was to it. He also wondered just how jealous Mikey Burns might have been. Mel might not be giving him the whole story.

"I know what you're thinking," Mel said. "You're thinking that Mikey killed Jerry because of me."

She sounded almost pleased that someone would come up with the idea, but not as if she believed it was possible.

"Do you think he did?" Rhodes asked.

"Not really. If Mikey had treated me right, he'd have dated me and maybe even more than that. But all he wanted to do was keep me on the string. If he'd cared enough about me to kill for me, he'd never have dumped me twice."

Rhodes thought she was right. Maybe there was nothing suspicious at all about her relationship with Kergan and Burns, though he still wasn't sure.

"Did you know the Crawfords?" he asked. "Larry and Terry. Twins."

"I don't think so. Do they have anything to do with computers?"

Rhodes doubted it. "They knew Kergan. Did you know much about his business at Dooley's?"

"All I know is that he was hoping to make a go of it. The restaurant business runs on a pretty narrow profit margin, so it's hard to get started and even harder to keep going. He was making it, but just barely."

"Do you know if he was doing anything to make a little extra money?"

"Like what? Something illegal?"

"Like selling moonshine whiskey," Rhodes said.

For the first time since he'd met her, Mel smiled. "You're joking, right? Moonshine whiskey? That sounds like something out of the thirties."

"It's still around," Rhodes said. "No pun intended."

"Pun?"

"Never mind. The Crawfords were making illegal whiskey on their property. I've heard they might have been selling it to Jerry Kergan."

Mel laughed. Rhodes was glad he was making her feel better. It was too bad he wasn't joking.

"I don't think so," she said. "I'd have known about it. I taught him how to do his accounts on the computer, showed him how to use spreadsheets. He didn't have anything set up for selling whiskey."

"He wouldn't," Rhodes said. "He'd know enough to keep that off the books."

"I guess he would. I still think I'd have known."

Maybe, maybe not, Rhodes thought. He thanked her for her help. Next, he'd go have a talk with Mikey Burns and see how the stories matched up.

He left Muller's manufactured home and got in the county car. Before he started for the precinct barn, he gave Hack a call to see if he was needed for anything else.

"You sure are," Hack said. "You need to drop by the Lawj Mahal. Randy Lawless wants to talk to you."

"What about?" Rhodes said.

"It ain't just him. It's him and another two guys."

"What two guys?"

"Larry Crawford," Hack said. "And Jamey Hamilton. You gonna go by there?"

"Call Lawless and tell him I'm on my way," Rhodes said.

FIFTEEN

THERE WAS PLENTY OF ROOM in the big parking lot in front of Lawless's large white office building. Rhodes parked right by the door.

He got out of the car and felt the heat reflected off the white walls. He stood for a second and looked over what remained of Clearview's downtown. There wasn't much. Only a few years ago, just about where the county car was parked, an old furniture store had stood, with a mural painted on its wall. Part of the town's Christmas celebration had been held on what was now the parking lot. Rhodes recalled the theft of the Baby Jesus that had occurred one year, and the death that had followed. It hadn't been one of the town's best celebrations, so maybe it was just as well that all the reminders had disappeared.

Rhodes shrugged off his thoughts and went inside the Lawj Mahal. The light was subdued, but the air was cool, almost cold after the heat in the parking lot. Rhodes wondered what Lawless's electric bill was, not that it mattered. Whatever it was, the lawyer could afford it.

Lawless's secretary said that Mr. Lawless was waiting, and she showed Rhodes into the inner sanctum. It was even nicer than Judge Parry's office. The law books lining the shelves were all bound in red leather, and the plush chairs were upholstered in leather of the same color. The pile of the rug was high enough to tickle Rhodes's ankles.

"Morning, Sheriff," Lawless said. He was sitting behind a

desk big enough to serve as a softball field in a pinch. "I think you know my clients."

Sitting in two of the big red chairs were Jamey Hamilton and Larry Crawford. Crawford was dressed pretty much as he'd been when Rhodes had last seen him, but the T-shirt was different. It said I'M ON DEBT ROW in red letters.

No doubt Crawford didn't have much of a wardrobe left after the explosion of the trailer, Rhodes thought, so he must have bought some more clothes. Except that the ones he was wearing didn't look new.

Hamilton was much younger than Crawford. He had black hair, blue eyes, and a smooth face. Rhodes wondered who was running the barbershop. Maybe Hamilton didn't have many customers and didn't have to stay open for long hours. But that couldn't be right, not according to what Michal Schafer had said.

"Hey, Sheriff," Crawford said. "You found the man who killed my brother yet?"

"How did you know he'd been killed?"

"Mr. Lawless told me. How do you think? So did you find who killed him?"

"Not yet," Rhodes said. "But I will."

"I bet. I told Jamey you would."

"Hey, Sheriff," Hamilton said. "That's what he was telling me all right."

"I want that son of a bitch," Crawford said. "Whoever he was, you better find him before I do. Nobody's gonna kill my brother and get away with it."

"Have a seat, Sheriff," Lawless said, ignoring Crawford's comment. "We have a few things to discuss."

"We do at that," Rhodes said. "Jerry Kergan would be one of them."

"What?" Lawless said. He'd been leaning back in his chair,

relaxed and at ease, but at the mention of Kergan's name, he sat forward. "What about Jerry Kergan?"

"He's dead," Rhodes said. "And then there's the whiskey still."

"I know about Mr. Kergan," Lawless said. "I was sorry to hear it, but I don't see what his death has to do with my clients."

"Maybe nothing," Rhodes said. "The whiskey still does, though." He looked at Larry, who avoided his eyes. "With one of them anyway."

"That's what we need to talk about," Lawless said. He tapped a fingernail on his desk. "My clients have nothing to do with the still, either."

Rhodes smiled. "It's on Larry's property."

"That might be true," Lawless said. He smiled, too, but he didn't mean it any more than Rhodes had. "That doesn't mean it's his still. It belonged to Terry."

There were times when Rhodes just wanted to laugh and say "Nice try." This was one of them. However, being a professional lawman, he always managed to restrain himself, even though it wasn't easy.

Lawless must have seen the amusement in Rhodes's eyes, but that didn't keep him from going on with his story.

"We think that's why Terry wasn't in the house when it exploded," the lawyer said. "He must have been going down to the creek to check on his still. We think someone was waiting for him there and shot him."

Rhodes wondered who had told Lawless where Terry's body had been found. Rhodes hadn't told him, but it didn't matter. The whole story would all be in the report that Rhodes had written, and Lawless would get a copy of it sooner or later. The report, however, would say that Terry had been shot at the house, not down by the creek. Rhodes could have mentioned that, but he didn't.

Rhodes wondered about the "we" Lawless had mentioned.

Did Lawless really expect Rhodes to believe that Crawford had come up with that idea on his own? Probably not. It was all part of the game to Lawless.

"You might want to save the story about the still for the TABC rep when he gets here," Rhodes said. "I'm not going to arrest Larry for the still. I'll let the TABC handle that."

Rhodes could have arrested Crawford, because local officials often cooperated with the TABC, and Rhodes planned to do so this time. But he didn't want to make an arrest without having the TABC agent take a look at the evidence.

"Nobody's going to arrest Larry," Lawless said. "After all, it wasn't his still."

"Terry'd tell you the same, if he was here to do it," Larry said. "I tried a hundred times to convince him to get rid of it, but he never listened to me."

"There'd been some trouble about the still," Lawless said. "Not between the brothers. This was something else."

While Rhodes usually got impatient with the same old spiel, he was always glad to hear something new, or even a variation on a theme.

"What kind of trouble?" he asked.

"I'll let Larry tell you about it," Lawless said. "Go ahead, Larry."

Rhodes had already suspected that there had been some coaching going on. Now he was absolutely convinced of it.

"Well, Sheriff," Larry began, "like I said, I tried to tell Terry that still of his was gonna get him in trouble. There's some folks don't like stills."

"The folks in the sheriff's department and at the TABC sure don't like them," Rhodes said, though he was pretty sure Larry wasn't talking about those people.

"I don't mean the law," Larry said, confirming Rhodes's suspicions.

"Who are you talking about, then?"

Larry looked at Lawless, who gave him a little nod. You can't beat a good coach, Rhodes thought. Larry looked back at the sheriff.

"Vigilantes," he said.

ACCORDING TO THE STORY Larry told, he and Terry had been getting "anonymous threats."

"We got these notes," he said. "Printed on white paper, like by a computer. They said stuff like 'If you don't stop what you're doing, we'll stop you ourselves.' That's why I was telling Larry he had to quit making whiskey. Besides it being against the law, I mean."

"I'd like to see the notes," Rhodes said.

"Well, see, they all got burned up when the trailer exploded," Larry said. "Otherwise, I'd be happy to show 'em to you."

Rhodes wondered if Larry had ever told a teacher that his dog had eaten his homework, but he had to give Larry credit. Or maybe Lawless should get the credit. At any rate, it was easy enough to claim that the notes had existed and that the explosion had destroyed them. Nobody could prove otherwise.

"If you want to know what I think," Larry continued, "I think it was that Benton fella and some of his friends. He's been spying on me and Terry, I can tell you that. He's said a few things around town about how he'd like to get rid of us. Like he's the king of the world or something."

Larry had called Benton a "nosy asshole," Rhodes recalled. He wondered just how far Benton's nosiness had gone. He also wondered about the pickup that had tried to run him down. Could it have been driven by vigilantes who'd come to take out the still?

The problem was that Rhodes didn't want to believe in the vigilante idea. It was like something out of the Old West, from some old black-and-white movie with Randolph Scott or Joel

McCrea. Judge Parry would believe it, though. He'd even come up with the same idea. As much as Rhodes hated to admit it, maybe there was some truth to the possibility.

"It's an interesting thought," he said, "but I'm not the one you should be telling it to. Somebody from the TABC will be here later today. You can talk to him."

"I don't want to talk to him." Larry looked to his lawyer. "Will I have to?"

"Not for a while," Lawless said. "If ever."

"Maybe I'd just better arrest you right now," Rhodes said. "To be sure you talk to him. We found some whiskey at that still, and you made it."

"No, he didn't make it," Lawless said.

He sounded confident, and Rhodes wondered why. Then he remembered: no fingerprints.

"You don't have to worry about Larry running off, Sheriff," Lawless continued. "And you don't have to worry about the TABC, Larry. You're completely innocent. Your late brother will have to shoulder the blame."

That's going to be pretty hard for Terry to do, Rhodes thought, considering where he is. Rhodes had to admit that it was a good ploy, about the only one Larry had. Blame the dead man. Lawless could probably drag it out in the courts for years. That is, he could if Larry had the money to pay him, which seemed pretty unlikely.

Unlikely, that is, unless there was a big settlement for the explosion that had taken out the manufactured home. Terry hadn't died in it, so wrongful death was out of the picture, at least for the propane company. That didn't mean that Larry couldn't collect the value of his home, plus some damages, however. Lawless must have thought that was a good possibility, or he wouldn't have Larry for a client. Rhodes needed to talk to Chief Parker to see if he'd finished his investigation into what caused the explosion. If he had, Rhodes wanted to know what he'd found out.

However, he didn't want to discuss any of that at the moment. He had something else on his mind.

"Let's talk about Jerry Kergan," he said.

"I don't think my clients have anything to say on that subject," Lawless told him.

"You know he was murdered, don't you?"

"I heard that he'd been killed, but I'm not sure murder was mentioned. I don't see any connection between that and my clients anyway."

"They knew him, or one of them did. Pretty well, I've heard. Right, Larry?"

"I knew him," Larry said, looking down at the thick carpet as if it were the most fascinating thing he'd seen in years. "We were friends. Terry and me grew up around Thurston, and we knew him there. We ate at his place once or twice, talked over old times. That's about it. We weren't real close buddies or anything."

Lawless stood up. "You don't have to talk about Jerry Kergan, Larry. The sheriff is just fishing around. Unless he's going to arrest you for something or other, I think he should go now."

Rhodes didn't mind leaving at that point. He at least knew more now than when he'd come in. He had only one more thing he wanted to say.

"I have a question for you," he said to Lawless. "It's about these vigilantes Larry thinks were after him."

"I wouldn't know anything about them."

"You were in our Citizens' Sheriff's Academy, though. You know the others who were in the class. Benton, for one. Did you ever hear any of them talking about Larry and Terry and what they suspected them of?"

"Not a word," Lawless said. "If the others talked about things like that, they knew better than to do it in front of a lawyer. A couple of them were lawyers, too. Well, one of them was."

"Not in Texas," Rhodes said, thinking of Max Schwartz.

"A lawyer's a lawyer," Lawless said. "They train us well. We all think alike."

"Now there's a scary thought."

Lawless nodded. "I'd have to go along with that. Now, don't you have some important sheriff business to do? What about that book signing at the Wal-Mart? I was planning to get you to sign a copy for me."

"I might not be there," Rhodes said. "I'm sure the authors will be more than happy to sign a book for you if I can't make it."

"It wouldn't be the same."

"You'd get over it."

"Yes," Lawless said, "I guess I would."

SIXTEEN

MOST SMALL COUNTIES in Texas weren't lucky enough to have a doctor trained in forensic pathology living in them. As a result, they shipped bodies that required an autopsy to the medical examiner in some nearby large city. This resulted in a big expense for the small counties, and it added more bodies to the huge backlogs that the bigger cities already had waiting for examination.

Blacklin County, on the other hand, had Dr. Alan White. He'd served his two-year internship after medical school and become certified as a forensic pathologist, only to decide that he didn't want to make examining dead bodies his career. He'd once told Rhodes that he preferred to deal with the living and to heal when he could, rather than probe into the secrets of the newly, and usually violently, dead.

However, Dr. White had been persuaded to take on the job of medical examiner for the county after he'd been assured that he could continue his private practice, since there would be few opportunities for him to do autopsies in such a small county. He was also promised that he wouldn't have to take any additional jobs from the neighboring counties if he didn't want to. With that assurance, he'd taken the job and had been doing it for years. He'd never taken any bodies from other counties, and he now insisted that if there was ever anything complicated or mysterious about a death, the body would have to be sent somewhere else for autopsy. Blacklin

County didn't have the facilities for anything other than routine work.

Rhodes didn't think there was anything too mysterious about the death of Terry Crawford, who'd simply been shot. So when he left the Lawj Mahal, Rhodes drove to the old redbrick mansion that now served as Clyde Ballinger's funeral home to see if the autopsy report was ready.

Rhodes couldn't remember when the funeral home had been anything other than what it was, but he'd heard stories about the old days, when one of the town's richest families had lived there and the grounds had occupied the entire block. There had been tennis courts and a swimming pool, a great rarity on private property in those days.

Now the place occupied only half a block. Big elm trees lined the lawn along the street, and a walk led up to a wide concrete porch that featured tall white columns.

Rhodes never went in the front door on business, however. He always drove around to the back, where Clyde Ballinger lived and had an office in the small building that had served as servants' quarters in the long-forgotten days when the mansion had been a family home instead of a funeral home.

Ballinger was in his office, reading, when Rhodes came in. There was nothing unusual about that. Ballinger nearly always had a book in his hand if he wasn't conducting business. It was the books themselves that were unusual, since Ballinger's choice of reading material was old paperbacks, preferably of the hard-boiled type written forty or fifty years earlier.

The funeral director looked up when Rhodes entered the office. Seeing who the visitor was, he held up the book so Rhodes could see the cover.

Rhodes was surprised. The book looked brand-new.

"I didn't know you bought new books," he said.

"I usually don't," Ballinger replied. He stood up and handed Rhodes the book. "Take a look."

Rhodes looked at the cover, which had an old-fashioned painting on it. The title of the book was *The Gutter and the Grave,* by Ed McBain. Rhodes knew that Ballinger was a big fan of McBain's 87th Precinct series, but the book didn't look as if it was about the cops Ballinger knew so well. Rhodes handed the book back to Ballinger.

"I thought McBain died a couple of years ago," he said. "I remember that you told me there wouldn't be any more books about the Eighty-seventh Precinct."

"That's right." Ballinger put the book on his desk. "This book's about a private eye. McBain wrote it nearly fifty years ago, but there's this publisher called Hard Case Crime that's reprinting books like that. Man, it sure beats finding them at garage sales." He picked up the book again. "Of course, it cost me six-ninety-nine, plus tax. I used to get 'em for a dime at garage sales."

"You could have waited till this one got old enough to show up at a garage sale," Rhodes pointed out.

"Couldn't wait. I'm getting old and impatient. You're as patient as ever, though, because I know you didn't come here to listen to me yammer about old books."

"Sometimes I think all I do in this job is listen to people yammer." Rhodes thought about Terry Crawford and Jerry Kergan. He thought about his shoulder and chest, which were still painful, even if they didn't hurt as much as before. "Now and then, there's a little bit more to it, though."

"Yeah, crime busting and all that. I might have to buy me another new book today just to read all about that kind of thing."

"You mean the one Claudia and Jan wrote?"

"*Blood Fever,*" Ballinger said. "Good title. Kind of gets you excited just hearing it. I bet the sheriff in that one's a real go-getter."

Rhodes wondered if that was a crack. He decided that it wasn't.

"He is. His name's Sage Barton. He's a crack shot and a devil with the women."

"Just like you," Ballinger said. "I hear you're the model for him."

"I don't know how stories like that get started. I just happen to know the authors. I've never been involved in the kind of things they're writing about. Just ordinary little murders like Terry Crawford's."

"Yeah. And I guess that's the reason you're here. Dr. White left the autopsy report for you. It's over here on my desk."

Ballinger put down *The Gutter and the Grave,* located the report, and handed it to Rhodes.

"Take a seat and read it over. Take your time. I'll read my book some more. I like the murders in books a lot better than real ones."

Rhodes wondered if Ballinger liked old books about murder and mayhem so much because he knew they weren't real. Maybe they helped him distance himself from the bodies he dealt with just about every day. Could be, he thought, but psychology wasn't his strong suit. He settled down to read the autopsy report.

It didn't take long, and the report pretty much confirmed what Rhodes had already guessed. Terry Crawford had died from two small-caliber gunshot wounds to the chest. Both bullets had remained in the body, and White said they were probably .25-caliber.

Rhodes thought using a .25-caliber pistol was about the same as throwing rocks, unless you were pretty close to the target. That meant that Terry had probably known his killer, or at least had let the person get close enough to shoot with some accuracy. But not too close. There were no powder burns on the T-shirt Terry had been wearing.

The bullets had tumbled in Terry's body and one had nicked his heart. Rhodes was surprised he'd gotten as far from the house as he had.

Another thing: Dr. White thought that Terry had bled so much because he'd been moving, maybe running. Rhodes wondered what Terry was running from.

Then there was the pistol. A small pistol like a .25 is a shop-keeper's gun, Rhodes thought, something like Max Schwartz might keep under the cash register. Or something like Jerry Kergan might have had in the restaurant.

Of course, it was also the type of pistol someone might buy at a flea market, the kind of thing you could easily conceal, even carry in a pocket.

"Dr. White left the bullets for you," Ballinger said when Rhodes looked up from reading the report. "You want to go get them?"

Rhodes nodded, and they left the office for the back room of the mansion, where the autopsy room was located. Rhodes got the bullets from the locker where Dr. White had put them. They were in a plastic bag with a label on it. White had printed the label so it could be read easily, not that his handwriting was as bad as people joked it was.

"What about Jerry Kergan?" Ballinger asked. "Why no autopsy on him?"

"We know how he died," Rhodes said. "No question about it. I was practically there when it happened."

"Too bad about him," Ballinger said. "I thought he was going to make a go of that place and get himself set up pretty well."

"Maybe," Rhodes said. "We'll never know now."

"I guess not," Ballinger said.

AFTER LEAVING the funeral home, Rhodes drove by the fire station, a brand-new building located across the street from the old fire station. Some of the old-timers remembered a third fire station, which had been located a couple of blocks down the street, but that building, like so many others in Clearview's downtown, was long gone, whether having been demolished or having crumbled on its own, Rhodes didn't know.

Chief Parker was sitting on a bench in front of the station, as if he'd been waiting for the sheriff to come by. Rhodes drove into a spot at the side of the building. He got out of the car and joined Parker on the bench, but not before admiring the big red engines in the bays.

"You ever think about being a fireman when you were a kid?" Parker asked when Rhodes sat down.

"All the time. I used to listen for the sirens and beg my daddy to take me to see the fires, but it wasn't the fires I cared about. It was the engines. What about you?"

"Never thought about it," Parker said. "I wanted to be Mr. October, hitting home runs in the World Series, not investigating explosions in manufactured homes."

"But here you are."

"Yeah. I like doing this job, too. Now that I'm here, I don't think I'd want to be doing anything else, even hitting those home runs. I trained a long time for this."

"You have plenty to do with this drought."

"More than enough," Parker said. "We've already been out on a call this morning. Nothing serious."

"Did you get to look over what's left of the Crawford place?"

"I went out there. I heard about Terry Crawford, too. I don't think I can help you with him, since he wasn't killed in the explosion."

"I know how Terry died. Right now, I'm more interested in what happened to his house."

"I'm sure it was a propane explosion," Parker said. "I even have the part of the pipe linkage that might have been responsible. That leaves us with a lot of other questions, though."

"What questions?" Rhodes asked.

"Why didn't anybody smell the gas? Propane has ethyl mercaptan in it so people will have warning, just like natural gas."

"Nobody was there to smell it," Rhodes said. "Larry was at Wal-Mart buying groceries, and Terry must have been outside."

"For how long? The gas must have built up in the house."

Rhodes didn't know how long. "I guess he was outside for a good while, then."

"Okay, if he was outside, what caused the explosion? Gas doesn't just combust by itself. There has to be a flame or something to ignite it. If there wasn't a flame, there had to have been a spark or something."

Rhodes didn't have an answer for that, either. He said he'd have to ask Larry Crawford.

"He's planning a lawsuit," Rhodes said. "How will what you found affect that?"

"Could be some carelessness on Larry's part, or Terry's. The manufacturer will say so. It'll come down to who has the best lawyers."

"Larry has Randy Lawless."

"He's the best from around here, for sure. The propane company or the home manufacturer, or both of them, will get somebody just as good. Lawless might get a settlement without ever going to court, though. Sometimes that's the easiest way for the defendants."

Rhodes figured that's what Lawless was hoping for, and Larry, too.

"Could be a good settlement, too," Parker continued. "Inflate the value of the house, put in a good bit for pain and suffering. Larry would've gotten the key to the mint if Terry'd been in there."

Getting a big settlement would make Lawless very happy, Rhodes thought. The lawyer liked nothing better than winning a case or settling one that brought him a lot of notoriety and got his name in the local paper. If it got his name in the city papers, too, so much the better.

"It doesn't matter much to Terry either way," Rhodes said. "Him being dead and all."

"I heard Jerry Kergan was killed, too. Some kind of hit-and-run. You catch who did it?"

Rhodes wished people would quit asking him that.

"I will," he said. "Sooner or later."

"Seems like you always do."

"Me and the Mounties," Rhodes said. "We always get our man."

SEVENTEEN

RHODES HAD MISSED lunch again. He'd planned to eat and then go by and talk to Mikey Burns, but when he took the bullets by the jail and put them in the evidence locker, Hack told him that he had other things to do. Like going to Wal-Mart for the book signing.

"I had to send Ruth out there for crowd control," Hack said. "Cars all over the place."

That didn't sound good, so Rhodes figured he'd better go and check on things.

"You plannin' to stick around, sign some books?" Hack asked.

Rhodes said he didn't know.

"If you do, you be sure to bring me and Lawton one apiece. We can read, you know."

Hack liked to watch TV at the jail, and Rhodes had never seen him with a book. However, he said he'd try to get a couple of copies.

"Better fill out this form, too," Hack said. "Vacation time. Don't want anyone to say you're doin' personal stuff on the county's time."

Rhodes filled out the form, wondering when he'd ever had an actual vacation. It had been years. He left the form with Hack and then drove to the highway, where he turned east toward the Wal-Mart.

Hack hadn't exaggerated. The parking lot was full, and cars were parked along the shoulder of the highway. Ruth Grady was doing her best to keep traffic moving and to stop people from parking on the highway itself. Either Wal-Mart was selling dollar bills for a penny or *Blood Fever* was going to be number one on the Clearview best-seller list.

Rhodes stopped beside Ruth and rolled down the window. "Are you going to be able to handle things here?"

"I think so." Ruth lifted her hat and wiped sweat off her forehead with her shirtsleeve. "Things have slowed down a little now. I've never seen anything quite like it. Vernell Lindsey's going to be jealous."

Vernell was a local romance novelist. She'd had some success with her signings at Wal-Mart, but nothing like this.

Rhodes left Ruth and drove through the packed lot, going around to the back of the building, where the automotive department was. He parked by a stack of new tires. He could smell the rubber when he stepped out of the car.

A man was changing tires on a truck in one of the bays. Rhodes told the man who he was and said that he was going to leave his car there for a few minutes.

"You better get on in the store, Sheriff," the man said. "I think they've been waiting for you."

Someone behind the cash register at the counter inside pushed the button that unlocked the door to the bays, and Rhodes went inside.

"They're all at the front of the store," the clerk said. "Sure are a lot of 'em."

Rhodes could hear the hum of conversation even where he was standing at the back of the store. He didn't know what to think about that, so he just started making his way through the aisles. He passed the electronics section, where the flat-screen TV sets were all showing a *Star Wars* DVD. Rhodes didn't know which episode it was.

He turned left to go up the wide aisle in the middle of the

store. He saw that the whole area up front was packed with people. There were so many of them that he couldn't see any of the checkout lanes.

Thelma Rice and Pearl Long, two members of the Older Women's Literary Society, were right in front. Rhodes wasn't surprised to see them. He'd spoken to the group once about a murder, and both women had expressed interest in *Blood Fever*. More interest than they'd expressed in the murder, as Rhodes seemed to recall.

Some of the members of the Red Hats were also there, right beside Thelma and Pearl. They weren't in their purple dresses and red hats, but Rhodes recognized them anyway. He'd spoken to that group about the murder, as well.

Shoulder-to-shoulder with them were Seepy Benton and Randy Lawless. Benton was wearing his hat, so he was easy to spot. Next to him was Jennifer Loam, her camera in hand.

Rhodes sighed.

Claudia and Jan stood behind a long table, their backs to him.

Thelma Rice spotted Rhodes. She pointed at him and called out, "Here comes the sheriff!"

Claudia and Jan turned around and saw him. They looked relieved.

"It's about time you got here," Claudia said when he arrived at the table. "We'd about given up on you."

She was a petite blonde with very blue eyes and a nice smile. She wasn't smiling now, however. Rhodes thought she might be a little miffed that he was late.

Jan was miffed, too, but she was trying not to show it. She gave him a quick smile that showed her dimples, and then asked him if he was ready to sign books.

Rhodes looked at the table in front of them. It was piled high with paperbacks. He thought there must be a hundred copies at least. Looking over the crowd, he wasn't sure that would be enough.

"We have more," Claudia said, as if reading his mind. She pointed to four cardboard boxes under the table. "Forty-eight books to a box."

Rhodes figured that would take care of any crowd you could draw in Clearview, but he didn't think he had time to sit down and sign that many books. Not that he had any right to sign them. He wasn't the author anyway.

The crowd was getting impatient. Four or five Wal-Mart employees in their blue vests were trying to make sure no one rushed the table.

"Everyone check to be sure you have your numbers," one employee said. "Nobody gets a signed book without a number."

"Numbers?" Rhodes said.

"They got numbers as they came in," Jan said. "They'll come to the table in order."

"We'd better sit down," Claudia said. "I hope all our signings are this good."

"They won't be," Jan said. "We won't have the main attraction with us."

"That's you," Claudia told Rhodes. "In case you didn't know."

The two women sat down, and Rhodes took a chair beside them. Jennifer Loam snapped a picture. Rhodes hoped he didn't look as addled as he felt.

Jan took a book off one of the stacks and handed it to him, telling him to see how he liked it.

The brightly colored cover showed a man who looked nothing at all like Rhodes. In fact, he looked a little like Terry Don Coslin, who had lived in Blacklin County and later become famous as a cover model for romance novels, including one Vernell Lindsey had written. Terry Don wasn't the man on the cover, however, because Terry Don was dead.

Not only did the man look nothing like Rhodes; he was wearing a large western-style hat and some kind of tight-fitting khaki uniform. Rhodes never wore a hat, and while the deputies were required to wear uniforms on duty, there was no such requirement for the sheriff.

The man on the cover—Sage Barton, no doubt—was crouched behind the open door of a car with a light bar on top. The light bar practically rippled with red and blue. Sage Barton was blazing away with a pistol that looked like a Frontier Model Colt .45 at three men running out of a bank building. The woman cowering behind Sage was dressed like Daisy Duke, except that her shorts might have been tighter.

"Good grief," Rhodes said.

"Isn't it great?" Jan said. "A cover like that will sell a lot of books for us."

"Very realistic," Rhodes said.

Jan gave him a sideways look. Rhodes tried to appear completely innocent.

"Open the book," Claudia said.

She helped him open it to the right place, the dedication page.

"Read it," Jan said.

Rhodes read the only lines on the page, which said, "This book is dedicated to Dan Rhodes, the handsome crime-busting sheriff of Blacklin County, Texas, without whose help and inspiration it would never have been written."

"Well," Rhodes said. He was flattered and surprised. "That's really nice. Thanks."

"You're welcome. Now you can see why we wanted you here. People will get a book signed by both authors and the person it's dedicated to. It will be a collector's item."

Rhodes didn't know about that. He just knew the whole thing was a little too much for him.

Claudia and Jan didn't give him time to think about that.

They said, "We're ready," and the Wal-Mart employee called out, "We're starting. Number one?"

"That's me!" Seepy Benton said, and he moved away from the crowd to the table.

What have I gotten myself into this time? Rhodes wondered.

HE WAS STILL wondering the same thing a couple of hours later, when all the books had been signed and most of the customers had gone home to read their purchases. Or to put them on the shelves to point out to visitors.

Jennifer Loam was still there, talking to Claudia and Jan and recording their comments on her little digital device.

Seepy Benton was there, too. He'd wandered off somewhere, but now he was back. Rhodes wasn't happy to see him.

"I've read a lot of the book already," he said. "I'm a speed reader, among other things."

Apparently, Benton is a good many things, Rhodes thought, but humble isn't one of them.

"I didn't realize you'd led such an exciting life," Benton continued. "I've been involved in crime busting, myself, and it was never quite like this."

He brandished the book to emphasize his point.

"Don't let the book fool you," Rhodes said. "It's never been quite like that for me, either."

"No need for false modesty," Benton said. "Anyway, I've been doing a little sleuthing around on the side today, and I think I can help you some more with our case."

"It's not *our case,*" Rhodes said. "I want you to keep out of it."

"What case?" Jan said, turning away from Jennifer Loam.

"Nothing," Rhodes replied.

"Murder," Benton said. "Murders, actually. Plural. Two of them."

"Why didn't you call us?" Jan said. She poked Claudia in

the back. Claudia turned around. "We need to hear about this. We might be able to use it in the next book."

"Next book?" Rhodes said.

"We got a two-book contract. We're working on number two now, but if the books sell, we're sure to get a contract for more. Now what's this about murders?"

"Yes," Claudia said. "What about them?"

Rhodes stood up. His hand was tired from giving out so many signatures, and he didn't plan to stay in Wal-Mart any longer.

"I'd like to introduce you to Seepy Benton," he said. He clapped Benton on the shoulder. "He can tell you all about it."

"Really?" Jan said.

"Really," Rhodes told her, and he turned to leave.

By the time Rhodes had taken two steps, Benton was in the chair the sheriff had vacated, leaning close to Jan to tell her all he knew.

EIGHTEEN

WHILE HE WAS signing books, Rhodes hadn't been thinking about what he was doing. He hadn't tried to think of a different inscription for each person; in fact, he hadn't used an inscription at all. His only problem had been deciding whether to sign "Sheriff Dan Rhodes" or simply "Dan Rhodes." He'd gone for the latter because it was shorter and he could get the books back to their owners faster.

So because he hadn't had to think about what he was doing, Rhodes had thought about the deaths of Terry Crawford and Jerry Kergan. He didn't doubt at all that the two were connected somehow. The black pickup was evidence enough of that. The problem was that he couldn't figure out exactly how they were connected. He couldn't come up with any real connection at all.

True, there were people who'd had it in for Crawford, but the same people wouldn't have had any reason, as far as Rhodes could see, to kill Kergan.

Both men had known some of the same people, and they'd known each other, but they hadn't known all of the same people. If they had, it might have made it easier to narrow down the suspects. And if only Rhodes could figure out who owned the black truck, things would become easier still. Rhodes thought the owner might be Jamey Hamilton, but he was far from sure. Buddy might have found out something about that, and Rhodes would check later. Right now, he was going to have that talk with Mikey Burns.

Driving toward the precinct barn, Rhodes considered what Seepy Benton had said. Was it possible that Benton really did know something important about the case? It didn't seem likely, but Rhodes regretted having walked away without at least talking to him for a minute or two.

If he hadn't been so worn-out from signing the books and so eager to leave Wal-Mart, Rhodes would never have acted as he had. Oh, well, he told himself, I can always talk to Benton later. He just hoped that Claudia and Jan wouldn't stick around town to add their help to Benton's. While one amateur helping out was bad enough, three would be intolerable. He was glad the two women had to move on and sign books somewhere else.

The trouble, he realized, was that the three of them no longer thought of themselves as amateurs. They'd all been part of the academy, so they all thought of themselves as professionals. Or, if not quite professionals, at least on the inside of things. They'd toured the jail. They'd seen the firing range. They'd done a ridealong. In their eyes, they were practically officers.

It seemed like a good idea at the time. The words echoed in Rhodes's head.

He told himself that the academy was still a good idea, that none of the students had been involved in what had happened to Crawford and Kergan, and that none of them would be a hindrance to his investigation. They'd all enjoyed the class, and they'd all be supporters of the department. The only problems seemed to be Benton and maybe Max Schwartz. Claudia and Jan didn't even live in the county, so they wouldn't cause any trouble. Judge Parry was wrong about the whole situation.

Or so Rhodes tried to convince himself. It wasn't easy, and all in all, he was glad when he arrived at the precinct barn, where he had other concerns.

When he went inside, Mrs. Wilkie picked up a copy of the book from her desk and held it up for him to see.

"I appreciate you signing this for me," she told him. I'm going to read it real soon now. I hear it's about you."

Rhodes didn't even remember signing a book for her, but so many people had been at the Wal-Mart that there was no way he could remember all of them. Some of them he'd hardly glanced at. He did recall that Ivy had been among the last fifty or so people who came by.

Ivy had told him that she was glad they'd used that old photo of him for the cover. He'd told her he was, too, and asked why she hadn't just let him bring a book home with him. She'd explained that she wanted to be there in person to see what being married to a celebrity was like.

Rhodes hadn't even smiled at that. He'd just handed her a couple of extra books and asked her to buy them for Hack and Lawton.

"The book's not about me," Rhodes told Mrs. Wilkie. "It's not even based on anything I've ever done."

"We'll see," she said. "I wonder if they say anything about the times I helped you out."

Mrs. Wilkie had more than once called Rhodes's attention to a couple of men who'd invaded Blacklin County and caused problems. Their names were Rapper and Nellie, and they claimed to be members of a motorcycle gang called Los Muertos, though Rhodes didn't think the gang really existed except in their imaginations. Just thinking about Rapper and Nellie made Rhodes nervous, but he didn't think they were around.

"Heard any motorcycles lately?" Rhodes asked her.

"No."

Rhodes relaxed a little.

"Are there any motorsickles in the book?" Mrs. Wilkie asked.

"Not a one," Rhodes said. "Is Mr. Burns here?"

"Let me check."

Mrs. Wilkie picked up the phone on her desk and pushed a button. Rhodes heard Burns answer, and Mrs. Wilkie told him that the sheriff would like to see him. After listening to a mumbled response, she hung up.

"You can go on in," she said, and Rhodes did.

Burns had on a different Hawaiian shirt today, one that was primarily green, white, and blue, with dolphins and waves. He also had a self-satisfied smirk on his face, and Rhodes was sure that couldn't be a good sign.

"Mrs. Wilkie tells me you've been doing personal business on county time," Burns said when Rhodes sat down. "That's something I'll have to mention at the next meeting of the commissioner's court. I hate to do it, but we can't have you cheating the taxpayers out of their money, can we?" He shook his head with mock sadness. "You need to be more careful, Sheriff. That's the kind of thing a man's opponent can use against him at election time, or maybe you don't think anybody'd dare to run against you."

Rhodes, who hated campaigning, had been unopposed in the last election, but he figured it might be time for someone to make another try at him. He was grateful that Hack had been looking out for him earlier.

"I signed those books on my own time," he said. "Filled out the right forms and everything to be sure I wasn't cheating anybody. You can call the jail and check if you want to. Better call now, so you'll know I did it earlier and didn't wait until after you reminded me."

Burns, who had been a little puffed up, deflated. His little smirk changed to a disappointed frown.

"I'm glad to hear it," he said. Rhodes could hear the lie in his voice, which didn't sound glad at all. "I don't need to call.

I don't doubt that you're a conscientious public servant and careful with the people's money."

Rhodes wondered again why Burns didn't like him. Part of it might have had to do with what had happened to Burns's predecessor, but surely that couldn't be the only thing.

"What about that Web site?" Burns asked, changing tactics. "Is it up and running yet?"

"No," Rhodes said. "But I'm glad you asked about it. That's the main thing I wanted to talk to you about."

Burns had worked up the beginning of a false smile, but even the trace of it disappeared, as if it had never been.

"Well," Rhodes went on, "not the Web site specifically. Mel Muller's what I really wanted to talk to you about."

"You did?"

"That's right. Jerry Kergan, too, while we're at it. I hear you were a pretty good friend of his."

"You hear a lot of stuff, don't you?" Burns said with a sullen look. "Always sniffing around, sticking your nose in, finding things out."

"It's what the taxpayers expect of me," Rhodes said. "I don't want to cheat them."

Burns glared at him. Rhodes answered the glare with a grin, and finally Burns dropped his eyes. They sat without speaking for a while, and then Rhodes said, "Why don't you tell me about your relationship with Mel Muller."

Burns opened his mouth, then closed it. He didn't say anything for a couple of seconds. Rhodes looked out the office window, hoping to catch a glimpse of a black Dodge pickup. A backhoe rumbled past, and that was all Rhodes saw.

"Did she tell you about us?" Burns asked when the backhoe was gone.

Rhodes didn't want to give anything away. "A little."

"She'd been dating Jerry Kergan, you know."

"Is that why you spent so much time in his office?" Rhodes asked.

Burns slumped in his chair. "Who told you that?"

"One of my sources," Rhodes said, hoping that made it sound as if he had hundreds of them.

"You don't have to tell me," Burns said. "It was that C. P. Benton. I know it was."

Rhodes just smiled.

"He saw me out there at that restaurant. He can't sing a lick, you know that?"

"I heard him last night. I thought he was pretty good."

"Well, that just shows you don't know anything about music. It was him who told you, wasn't it?"

Rhodes kept quiet.

"All right, I was there, and I talked to Kergan. It was strictly business, though. He's in my precinct, and I was checking to see if things were going all right for him. I like to keep in touch with the voters."

"Right," Rhodes said.

"So that's all there was to it. You have any more questions?"

Burns leaned forward, half-rising from his chair, plainly indicating that it was time for Rhodes to get up and leave. Past time, in fact. Rhodes sat right where he was.

"I do have a few more questions," he said. "You and Mel Muller were going together. You broke up and then took up again before Jerry Kergan started beating your time."

Burns balled his fists. "He wasn't beating my time. I wasn't even going with Mel anymore. If you think I killed Kergan because I was jealous of him and Mel or something like that, you're all wrong."

"I didn't even mention that he was dead."

"You're not tricking me, Rhodes. Everybody in town knows he's dead. You think something like that doesn't get around? I heard about it first thing this morning, and I was sorry to hear it. I hardly knew him, but I was sorry."

"And you never got upset with him because he was seeing Mel Muller?"

"Never. You think I'd have given her the Web site job if I was upset?"

"You didn't want to talk to her about it. You sent me to do it."

"Sure. It's your department. You should do the talking." Burns paused and rubbed his hand across his face. "All right. Maybe I would have felt a little awkward talking to her. What difference does it make?"

"None, probably," Rhodes said, "but you never know. The thing is that the Crawfords spent a lot of time with Jerry Kergan, too. So did you, and so did Mel Muller. I have to wonder what was going on in there."

"I don't know anything about the Crawfords. I was there on precinct business, like I told you, and that's it. That's all I have to say about it."

Rhodes knew better than to push it. He had a feeling that Burns would be on the phone to Judge Parry soon enough, complaining about his treatment by the mean old sheriff. It's a good thing my position is elective, he thought. I'd be fired within the hour if Burns had the power to do it.

Rhodes was sure that Burns had talked to Kergan about his relationship with Mel Muller. It appeared to Rhodes that Burns was still interested in Mel but didn't know how to do anything about it. Rhodes knew he wasn't as smooth with women as, say, Sage Barton, but he knew that confronting Kergan about his relationship with Mel was the wrong way to go about winning a woman's heart.

The best thing to come out of the conversation was that Burns most likely wouldn't be bothering him about that Web site again. Not anytime soon at least.

RHODES WENT BACK to the jail to meet with the representative from the TABC, who turned out to be Jack Mellon, a barrel-chested, no-nonsense lawman with whom Rhodes had worked on a couple of other occasions.

"How come you didn't bring me a book?" Mellon said when Rhodes handed copies to Hack and Lawton.

"I didn't think you'd be interested," Rhodes said.

"Mine's not signed," Lawton complained.

"Mine, neither," Hack said. "I can't take vacation time just on a whim like some folks, so I couldn't get out to the Wal-Mart, but I was expecting an autograph."

"I'll sign the books," Rhodes said. "I'm sorry I forgot."

Hack handed him a pen, and Rhodes signed the books.

"Don't read them while you're on the job," he said.

"I'm just gonna look at the cover," Lawton said. "That's a mighty good likeness of you."

"Yeah," Hack said. "Who's the woman? I don't remember seein' her around town."

"She just comes in for the bank robberies," Rhodes said.

He turned to Mellon and explained the situation with the Crawfords and told him the location of the still.

"So this Larry Crawford's claiming his dead brother was the sole owner and operator of the still," Mellon said.

"That's it. He swears he had nothing to do with it and that he tried to persuade Terry to stop making whiskey. By the time you meet him, he might be claiming he didn't even know the still was down there in the woods."

"If the land's in his name, or both their names, that might not matter. Is he where you can put your hand on him?"

"His lawyer's supposed to know where he is. We can find him when we want him."

"Let's go have a look at that still first," Mellon said.

"We can take my car," Rhodes told him.

AT THE GATE to the Crawford property, the chain was still locked around the post, and the fence was undisturbed. Rhodes felt good about that. He'd been a little worried that the chain would be cut or the fence would be down.

He got out of the car and keyed the lock, which snapped smoothly apart. Then he got back in the car and started to drive up the hill. The ruins of the manufactured home looked no better than they had the previous day, and having lain in the sun for hours, they were probably almost as hot.

Mellon wasn't interested in the wreckage, though. All he cared about was the still.

Rhodes drove up and over the hill, pointing out on the way down to the creek the spot where he'd found Terry Crawford's body. Mellon didn't care about that, either.

Rhodes stopped the car at the edge of the trees. "The still's about thirty yards in, under a little shed covered with camouflage netting."

The two men got out of the car, and although it was late afternoon, the heat was still powerful. Dead grass crackled under Rhodes's shoes. The walking didn't bother his chest or shoulder, but it did make him aware that he was still a little sore.

"How many stills have you ever found in this county?" Mellon said as they entered the trees. "Couldn't have been too many, not in a long time."

"This is the first one in years," Rhodes told him. He tried to remember the last time. It had been awhile. "Only two others, a good while back."

"You might find a few more than that this year, what with

white lightning coming back into style," Mellon said. "It's a fad, won't be around long, but somebody's going to make a dollar off it while it lasts."

They walked along, dead sticks cracking under their feet. When they came to the little shed, it was just as it had been on the previous day. The camouflage netting was also undisturbed.

The still, however, was gone.

"Looks to me like you haven't found one this time, either," Mellon said.

NINETEEN

THE TRACKS RHODES FOUND after looking around for a while
came from the direction of the creek. The dry grass was flattened
at the edge of the trees, where someone had parked, and there
was a spot of black oil the size of a large pancake on the ground.

Someone had driven a vehicle, which Rhodes was willing
to bet was a black Dodge pickup, along the nearly dry creek
and up into the woods, then loaded the still. Rhodes would have
to look for the place where the truck had left the road, but he
figured it was down by the bridge. Because there was no fence
between the Crawfords' property and the creek, it would have
been easy enough for someone to get to the still that way. Then
whoever it was had taken the still apart and carted it off. It would
take at least a couple of people to do that, Rhodes thought.

He'd made a mistake by overlooking the fact that someone
could come up to the trees by the back way, and it looked like
he'd been outsmarted. Mellon was too kind to say so, but
Rhodes could tell he was thinking the same thing.

"What with Crawford claiming he didn't own the still, and
what with the still being gone and all, I don't have much of a
case against him," Mellon said.

"We have pictures of the still," Rhodes said, remembering
that Ruth Grady had taken them. "Two of us saw it here and
can swear to it. That should be good enough for the court."

"It should," Mellon agreed, "and it probably would. I'm not
willing to make the arrest on that basis, though, not with this

Crawford fella ready to say the still wasn't his and having a high-powered lawyer to back him up. It's just not worth it. You can arrest him if you want to, but I don't recommend it."

"We have whiskey from the still," Rhodes said.

"Any proof that Crawford made it?"

Rhodes thought about the lack of fingerprints and said, "No."

"Then you're right back where you started."

Rhodes saw Mellon's point, but he didn't like it.

"Since this is a dry county," Mellon said, "if you catch him in possession, you'd have a case. One quart would do it if you were really out to get him."

Rhodes didn't think he'd be lucky enough to catch Crawford in possession, not now.

"Who do you think took the still?" Mellon said.

"Somebody driving a black Dodge," Rhodes told him, and then went on to explain what had happened when he and Ruth found the still. "Later on that night, the same truck killed a man named Jerry Kergan. So whoever was driving it is our man."

"Your man," Mellon said by way of correction and clarification. "Maybe it was Crawford."

"Could be, but we haven't been able to connect him to the truck so far. We haven't been able to connect anybody to it."

"You will. But as for the still, just forget it. Crawford might not even own this property. If he doesn't, you'll really be on shaky ground. Anyway, you have two murders on your hands. That's enough."

Though he didn't say so, Rhodes didn't agree. He wanted to get Larry Crawford for the still, too. It didn't seem right that he should get away with making illegal alcohol.

That thought reminded him again of Rapper and Nellie, both of whom had gotten away with a lot in Blacklin County, maybe even murder.

Not that they'd gotten off scot-free. Once, Rapper had lost a couple of fingers in a fight with Rhodes. Another time, both he and Nellie had wound up in the hospital, Nellie with broken ribs and Rapper with a severe thigh wound, the result of another fight with Rhodes, who had sunk the sharp point of a hay hook in him.

Rapper and Nellie, however, hadn't learned much from those encounters. They'd returned to the county one more time, and Rhodes had been in yet another fight with Rapper, who that time had gotten most of one ear shot off.

Each time, however, Rapper had come close to getting the better of Rhodes. He'd outthought him and outmaneuvered him on more than one occasion.

Why do I keep thinking about him? Rhodes wondered. He and Nellie are motorcycle guys. They don't drive trucks.

"We might as well go on in," Mellon said. "We're not going to find anything else here."

Rhodes thought about following the tracks, but he decided to come back later. No need to delay Mellon's return to his home base. They went to the car, and Rhodes drove them back to town.

AFTER MELLON HAD LEFT, Rhodes checked with Hack to see what was going on with the donkey at the car wash, among other things.

"Franklin Anderson took care of him," Hack said. "Got him roped and penned up without much trouble. Didn't find out who owned him, though."

Rhodes wasn't worried about that. The owner would be calling sooner or later.

"Could be a mule," Lawton said, walking into the room from the cell block.

"Anderson says it was a donkey," Hack told him. "Just like I thought."

Rhodes didn't recall that, exactly, but he kept quiet. He didn't want to get them started again.

"Anderson didn't do anything about those possums, though," Hack said.

"We're working on it," Rhodes told him.

"Right. That's what I told Miz Owens, just like you said. I've had to tell her twice since the first call. I don't think she took any comfort from hearin' it."

"It's the best I can do right now. What else is going on?"

Rhodes hoped that Hack would say "Nothing," but that had never happened before. Something was always going on.

"Buddy called in about that Jamey Hamilton. He can't find out a thing on him except that he cuts a lot of hair."

"I knew that already."

"Buddy says it's kind of suspicious how much hair he cuts. Lots of folks in and out of that shop. More than you'd think for a little town like Obert."

Rhodes recalled what Michal Schafer had told him.

"Does Buddy think something else was going on?"

"He's checkin' some more, but he says it might be that Hamilton was sellin' liquor out of the shop."

Rhodes wanted to get some evidence of that and tie it back to Larry Crawford, though it wasn't likely that anyone who'd bought liquor there would admit it.

"Tell him to keep working on it. Anything else?"

"Dave Ellendorf phoned," Hack said.

Rhodes sighed. Ellendorf was a well-known nutcase. "What's the trouble this time?"

"I bet it's the flyin' saucers again," Lawton said, earning a hostile look from Hack.

"Is it?" Rhodes asked.

"Yeah," Hack said, still looking at Lawton.

"What are they up to this time?"

Hack looked back at Rhodes and grinned. "Stealin' his 'lectricity."

No wonder Hack's mood had improved so quickly. That was a completely new story from Ellendorf. On previous occasions, Ellendorf had variously claimed that the flying saucers—black ones, of course—were spying on him, trying to abduct his two dogs, causing his chickens to stop laying, or making his house shift on its foundation.

After each of the calls, Rhodes had paid a visit with his special "saucer detector," which consisted of a couple of circuit boards from old transistor radios. No saucers had been detected, and Ellendorf had been happy. Until the next time.

"How does he know they're stealing his electricity?" Rhodes asked.

"Because it went off right after they flew over. He says they sucked all the 'lectricity right out of the house. He heard this high-pitched whinin' noise and went out in the yard. Saw four of those black saucers hoverin' over the house. Soon's he saw 'em, they whooshed straight up in the air and took his 'lectricity with 'em."

"Sounds serious," Rhodes said.

"Sure is," Lawton said. "Man without an air conditioner's in big trouble in weather like this."

"Did you tell him to call the electric company?" Rhodes asked.

"Nope. I figured you'd better go out and have a look first. Takes the 'lectric company too long to do anything anyway. It might be tomorrow before they got somebody out there. If it's something you can't solve, you can tell him to give 'em a call. They might get there in a couple of hours, or it might be a couple of days. Depends on what else they got to do."

"All right," Rhodes said. "I'll see if I can take care of him. Then I might drive down to Thurston to have a look at Jerry Kergan's house."

"He had an apartment here in town now."

"He still owned his place in Thurston, didn't he?"

"Far's I know."

"Then I need to have a look around. You get in touch with Ruth and have her check the apartment."

"You be sure to let me know where you are," Hack said.

"I will."

"Ruth always lets me know where she is."

Rhodes ignored the implied criticism and started for the door, but Seepy Benton came in before he got there.

"We need to talk, Sheriff," he said.

"What about?"

"The Crawfords. I told you I knew a few things that might be important."

"All right," Rhodes said. "Come on over to the desk."

He sat at his desk and Benton sat beside it in an old wooden chair that might have been new when the jail was built. He kept his hat on, but Rhodes didn't mind.

"Those authors I met today were really interested in our case," Benton said.

"Hold it," Rhodes said. "*Our* case?"

"Well, the one you're working on. I'm just a public-spirited citizen who'd like to help out."

"Right. Did you tell Claudia and Jan anything you haven't told me?"

"Two things. I'd have told you, but you didn't seem interested."

"I'm interested now."

"Good. The first thing's about the Schwartzes. I think you'd better question them again."

"Why should I do that?"

"I'm not sure I should say."

Rhodes stood up. "And you have every right not to. I have some things I need to do anyway."

Benton grinned. "I guess I asked for that. I came here to tell you, and then I didn't. I don't blame you for being a little irritated."

"He gets like that all the time," Hack said from across the room. "I don't know why he does."

Rhodes detected no trace of irony in his voice.

"Anyway," Benton said, "the Schwartzes were pretty upset with the Crawfords. They talked to a couple of us in the academy class about doing something about them."

"Why didn't you mention this before?"

"I didn't want them to get in trouble, and I didn't really think they were serious. That was before I heard the story of what Terry did in the store. I thought it was just about the meth lab, and—"

"There wasn't a meth lab," Rhodes said.

"If you say so. But we thought there was. I told them we couldn't do anything ourselves, that it was your job. You emphasized that in your class."

Rhodes was glad someone remembered. He'd been clear about citizens' responsibilities and how they differed from the responsibilities of the sheriff's department.

"I thought they agreed with me," Benton said. "They seemed to lose interest. Now I wonder if I was right. They were pretty upset, even now, about Terry Crawford."

"Does Schwartz keep a gun in his store?" Rhodes asked.

"I don't think so. If he did, Jackee might have used it on Crawford."

Rhodes hadn't thought of that. Jackee didn't look like the type, but he knew you could never tell what a person might do by looking at her.

"You said there were two things. What's the other one?"

"I saw somebody at the Crawford place today, at the gate."

"You've been watching it?"

Benton stiffened, as if he'd been insulted.

"Watching? No. I just happened to look up that way when I was leaving home this morning."

Rhodes didn't think Benton could see the gate from the road in front of his house, but it might be barely possible.

"What did you see?"

"A black truck. There were two men in it."

Rhodes hadn't been too sure of the accuracy of the information about the Schwartzes, but this was more interesting.

"Could you tell what they looked like?"

"Not until they got out of the truck. The windows were too dark."

"Well?" Rhodes said.

"One of them was short and hefty. Not fat, but he had a big belly. It looked solid, like a barrel."

"Did he walk with a limp?"

"How did you know?"

"Call it a lucky guess. What about the other one?"

"Skinny, wore a baseball cap, black jeans, and a black T-shirt."

Rapper and Nellie. No wonder Rhodes had been thinking of them. Maybe he'd recognized them in the truck without even realizing it.

"You can really see well from your place," Rhodes said. "Do you have binoculars?"

"No. After I saw them, I drove up that way instead of coming to town." Benton put up a hand. "I wasn't investigating. I didn't put myself in any danger. I was just doing what a responsible citizen would do."

"You're right," Rhodes said. "This county needs more responsible citizens who're ready to help out law enforcement now and then."

"I'm always happy to help out," Benton said.

"Good," Rhodes told him. "Because I have a little job for you."

TWENTY

"THAT WAS A PRETTY mean trick," Hack said when Benton was gone.

Rhodes shook his head. "He said he wanted to help."

"Yeah," Lawton said. "Maybe so, but I don't think he knows much about possums."

"What's there to know?" Rhodes said. "He goes up in the attic and chases them out. One citizen helps out another."

"Miz Owens won't like it," Hack said.

"Sure she will. She just wants to get rid of the possums. She doesn't care who does the job."

"She asked for you, though."

"She'll like Benton. Everybody does."

"He did seem like a nice fella," Lawton said. "Maybe he'll bring his guitar around and give us a concert."

Benton had mentioned his guitar playing before leaving. He always manages to work it into the conversation, Rhodes thought.

"I'd like to hear him," Hack said.

"We work here," Rhodes reminded them. "This is a jail, not a music hall."

"Irritable," Hack said, turning to Lawton. "Like I said."

"Kinda sad," Lawton said. "He didn't use to be like this."

Rhodes left before they could say any more.

DAVE ELLENDORF looked like a perfectly normal guy. He was nearly seventy, with white hair so thin that Rhodes could see the pink skin of his scalp. He wore glasses and baggy pants that slid down and lapped over the tops of his shoes because of the belly that pooched out over his belt. Not that there's anything wrong with that, Rhodes thought, reminded that he couldn't always be sure of seeing his own belt buckle.

Appearance aside, however, there was something distinctly odd about Ellendorf, and it wasn't just his belief that black flying saucers were hovering around and stealing his electricity. It had something to do with his high-pitched voice and the way he never quite looked directly at whomever he was talking to. His small eyes darted to the left and right and never stopped darting around.

"Where's your saucer detector?" he asked Rhodes first thing.

"I didn't think I'd need it," Rhodes said. "The saucers are gone, right?"

Ellendorf nodded. "Sure they are. They got what they wanted, and they were gone in a flash. Sounded like they'd been sucked right up into the sky in a big vacuum cleaner. Took that electricity with 'em, dammit."

"We'd better check," Rhodes said. "Maybe they brought it back."

"I didn't see 'em."

"They're sneaky, though."

Ellendorf thought that over. "I guess you're right about that. But the electricity's still gone. I'll show you."

The house was small, and it was located just outside the city limits. There was a fenced chicken yard in back, and a couple of dogs slept in the shade on one side of the house.

Ellendorf took Rhodes into the cramped one-car attached garage, leading him past an old Ford Escort that was red, faded, and dusty. Its nose almost touched the door to the interior of the house. There was a dirty plastic light switch beside the door, and Ellendorf flipped it up. The light didn't come on.

"See?" he said.

"What about the rest of the house?"

"I'll show you that, too."

Ellendorf opened the door. They went into a utility room that was almost too small for the washer and dryer it held. Ellendorf flipped the light switch on the wall by the door. Nothing happened.

"No air-conditioning, either," he said. "Mighty damn hot in here."

Rhodes had to agree that it was. "You've been running that AC day and night, I guess."

"Damn right. Too hot not to. Got it cranked right down to seventy-four, too. I say to hell with that 'keep it on seventy-eight' crap they keep preaching. A man wants to be cool in this weather."

Rhodes went back into the garage. It must be about 120 in here, he thought. He looked across the top of the Escort to the opposite wall and saw the gray metal door of the circuit-breaker box.

He went around the back of the Escort and slipped sideways along the side of the car so he could get to the breaker box. He pulled on the silver ring and opened the door.

Sure enough, the main breaker had been tripped. Ellendorf had strained his electrical system.

Rhodes flipped the breaker back on. He heard an air-conditioner compressor kick in somewhere behind the house, and the garage light came on.

Ellendorf came into the garage. "They brought it back! How'd you make 'em do it?"

Rhodes explained about the breaker and told Ellendorf to turn up the thermostat. "And you'd better call the electric company. Have them come out and check your electrics. You might want to call an air-conditioner repair place, too. Get your whole system checked."

"Costs money," Ellendorf said. "Those E.T.s'd just come back and steal my electricity again."

"I have something that might keep them away," Rhodes said. "An E.T. repeller."

"You shoulda brought that before."

"I just got it. I'll bring it by tomorrow."

"You think it'll help?"

"It's guaranteed," Rhode assured him.

"All right, then. I'll try to stand it with the AC temp turned up a little."

"You do that," Rhodes said.

He left Ellendorf standing there looking up at the hot blue sky.

THURSTON WAS A TOWN that had fallen on hard times. It had always been small. Now it was almost nonexistent: one grocery store, and not much else.

The owner of the store was Hod Barrett, a short, stout, solid man with red hair stiff as brush bristles. And a temper. He'd never been one of Rhodes's supporters, and he didn't much like seeing the sheriff in his store.

"You oughta be out solvin' crimes," Barrett said. "Not stoppin' by here for a Dr Pepper."

Rhodes sat on the wooden bench in the front of the store. The boards had been worn smooth by generations of customers who'd sat there, just as Rhodes was now, drinking Dr Pepper in glass bottles and eating MoonPies.

Rhodes had the Dr Pepper, and he wished he had a MoonPie, but even missing lunch didn't mean he could splurge like that, or so he told himself.

"I'm here on business," he said. "In fact, that's why I stopped here." He held up the Dr Pepper for Barrett to admire. "The drink's just a bonus for me."

The interior of the store was dim and cool. The high ceilings helped, and Rhodes liked to look at the pattern of the stamped tin. He wondered how old that ceiling was. Older than either he or Barrett, for sure.

"What'd you want to ask me?" Barrett said. "I got customers to wait on."

Rhodes looked around the store. He didn't see any customers. He doubted that any would come in. Thurston was just about dead.

"I make deliveries," Barrett said, as if he could tell what Rhodes was thinking. "Lots of folks here can't get out and shop for themselves, so they call in their orders. They've got old, need somebody to help them out. I don't charge 'em anything for the deliveries."

"I won't bother you long," Rhodes said, a little surprised, though he shouldn't have been, that Barrett was willing to help people. Things like that still happened in small towns, maybe even in cities, but you never heard about them. "I want to ask you about Jerry Kergan."

"Him," Barrett said in a tone that indicated a low opinion of the man. "He moved off to Clearview to get rich. Couldn't make it here. Not enough business. I guess you can figure out why."

"Not many people left in town," Rhodes said. "There are still some out in the country and down by the lake, though."

"Yeah," Barrett said. "But not many."

Rhodes noticed the scant stock on the store shelves and wondered how much longer Barrett would be able to keep his store open. What would happen to those people who needed deliveries when it closed?

"Kergan still had a house here, didn't he?" Rhodes asked.

"Yeah," Barrett said. "I think maybe he rented it out to somebody."

Rhodes hadn't heard that. "You know he was killed last night?"

"Ever'body in town knows about that." Barrett gave Rhodes

a crooked grin. "Heard you were right there when it happened and didn't do a thing to stop it."

Rhodes thought that Barrett would have been a happy man if the sheriff had been crushed instead of Kergan.

"I wasn't in much of a position to stop it," Rhodes said.

"Yeah."

Barrett's tone implied that he didn't believe a word of it. Rhodes didn't challenge him.

"Who rented Kergan's house?" he asked, taking a sip of the Dr Pepper.

"Now that's kind of funny," Barrett said. He rubbed a hand across his bristly head. "Not ha-ha funny. You know. The other kind."

"What's funny about it?"

"I pass by there now and then making deliveries, and I see signs that somebody's around, but I never see who it might be. Maybe it's not rented out after all. People been messing around there, though."

"You should have called my office if you were suspicious that something like that was going on."

"Huh."

Barrett was able to put a lot of meaning into a single sound. Rhodes interpreted it as "Fat lot of good that would do."

"Where's the house located?" Rhodes asked.

"On the road going to the Plunkett Cemetery," Barrett said. "You know where that is?"

"Not far from the old Gin Tank," Rhodes said.

Once, Thurston had been a cotton town, with two or three cotton gins running day and night at cotton-picking time. That had been a long time ago. There were no cotton fields around Thurston anymore, and hardly a trace of the gins remained. A big pond, called the Gin Tank, had been near one of them, and though the gin was gone, the pond still had the same name.

Probably only a few people in the town even remembered how it had gotten it.

"That's right," Barrett said. "Go around the curve by the tank, and it's the first house you see on the right."

Rhodes thanked him, finished the Dr Pepper, and left.

TWENTY-ONE

THE AIR FELT a little cooler to Rhodes when he got out of the car in front of Kergan's house, but that was likely because it was late in the afternoon and the sun was coming at him from a slant instead of bearing down from directly overhead. The actual temperature hadn't changed much.

The Gin Tank wasn't far from the house. Willow trees grew all around it, and Rhodes couldn't see the water. He hoped that the tank hadn't gone dry. He liked to think that the water shielded by the willows was still and green and cool, that lunker bass swam in the weeds near the banks, waiting for someone to toss in a lure.

He knew better than that, however. He'd talked to more than one rancher who'd had to shoot a cow that had bogged down in the mud while trying to reach the small pool of water that was in the middle of the tank.

There'd been a time when the tank was full, though, and Rhodes would have tossed in a lure if he'd gotten the chance. He wished he had more opportunities to go fishing. It seemed as if he had none at all lately, and unless there was a gully-washing rain, he wouldn't have any for a long time to come.

He looked at Kergan's little white frame house. It was deserted, and Rhodes thought no one had been there for a while. The grass was brown and dry. A couple of dead rosebushes grew in what had once been a flower bed.

There were no near neighbors, and not another house was

in sight. Fields and pastures covered the land to the left and right, with only the Gin Tank and a few small wooded areas to break the monotony of brown weeds and grass. An occasional sprig of green stuck up, a weed that didn't know enough to die. If it doesn't rain soon, Rhodes thought, some of the old-timers will start talking about the Dust Bowl days.

Rhodes wondered about the renters that Barrett had mentioned. He didn't see any sign of them. If they'd ever been there, they were gone now.

A big sheet-metal shed sat about fifty yards behind the house. Rust stained the sides and top. It might have been used to store farm machinery at one time, maybe back when there were cotton fields. Rhodes wondered what might be inside it now.

He reached into his pocket and touched the Indian Head penny. He'd almost forgotten he had it with him. He didn't really believe in luck, but he did believe in the whimsical nature of things. He decided to let a flip of the coin decide whether he'd have a look inside the house first or walk back to the shed.

"Heads, it's the shed," Rhodes said aloud. He flipped the coin, and as it turned over and over, he said, "Tails, it's the house."

He snatched the coin out of the air with his right hand and slapped it down on top of his left wrist.

"Heads it is," he said.

He put the coin back in his pocket and walked toward the shed. As he did, he noticed that the grass around it had been flattened. Someone had been driving on it. Someone had been using the shed, possibly the renters that Barrett had mentioned.

The shed had a big metal door that slid along a track. There was a hasp at one end, but it wasn't fastened with a padlock through the staple. Rhodes didn't see any windows on the front of the shed, so he walked around to the side. He found a window all right, but it was too high for him to see through. A couple of panes were missing. Those that remained were covered with dust and dirt.

He went back to the front of the shed. He could either bang on the door and ask if anyone was inside or he could pull the door open and take his chances. He didn't like either idea, but he couldn't come up with a better alternative.

All three times when he'd dealt with Rapper and Nellie in the past, they'd found out-of-the-way places to stay: an abandoned house in one instance, tents in another. A shed like this would be a fine accommodation for them. It would be hot and all but suffocating. Rhodes wondered if anyone could stay inside for long.

In the shed's favor was its location. It was out of town, in a deserted part of the county. That was the kind of place Rapper and Nellie looked for every time.

Bending down, Rhodes took his .38 from the ankle holster. Then he banged on the door.

"Anybody home?" he called.

Nobody answered. Rhodes wasn't surprised. Using his left hand, he slid the door open.

It didn't slide easily. It squealed along the track, which dug into the ground beneath it. After it had slid a couple of feet, it stuck.

Rhodes looked at the hard dirt under the door and saw a long gouge. Someone had opened the door, probably recently. Rhodes could have forced it open farther, but he would have needed both hands to do it, and he didn't want to put away his pistol. So he stood outside, looking into the dim interior of the shed. A little light filtered in through the dirty windows and through the openings where the panes were missing, but not enough for Rhodes to see well.

He stood there for a couple of seconds, letting the heat from the inside stream over him while straining to hear any noise and waiting for any movement. It wouldn't have surprised him if Rapper and Nellie had suddenly appeared to open fire on him with automatic pistols, but the inside of the shed was quiet and still.

Rhodes was investigating property that belonged to a murdered man and therefore had ample cause to enter the shed without a warrant.

Nothing moved inside the shed except a few dust motes that floated through the sunlight coming in through the space where the panes were missing. If Nellie and Rapper had been there, they were gone now. Rhodes put his pistol back in the holster and forced the door all the way open, letting more light into the building.

The shed had no floor other than the dirt its four walls sat on. The hulk of an old tractor sat near the back on one side. A wooden workbench was closer to the front. There might have been some old tools on it. Rhodes couldn't quite make them out. He walked over to have a look.

The workbench was old and had been there a long time. Its surface was pitted, rough, and dust-covered. A couple of rusty wrenches lay on it, along with a piece of a screwdriver. Rhodes thought they must have been left there years ago, not by Kergan, but by some previous owner of the property.

More interesting to him were the two cots that butted up against the wall under the broken window. Not far from them, a portable generator sat on the dirt floor. A fan was plugged into it. The fan was pointed toward the cots. It wouldn't keep anyone very cool, but it might make the place bearable at night, when the temperature would drop into the seventies.

Between the fan and the cots were three stacks of unmarked cardboard boxes. Rhodes didn't know what was in them, but he was going to look.

But the prize discovery was the still. It sat near the tractor, and, from where Rhodes stood, it appeared to be in good shape.

Whoever took it hadn't demolished it. It had just been moved from one place to another.

Leaning against the hot metal wall near the still was a stack of bulging burlap bags. Rhodes could smell the corn chops from where he stood. He walked over and kicked the bottom bag with his toe. Dust rose from it, along with the strong smell of the corn chops.

Rhodes took a look at the tractor, which was at least as old as the tools on the workbench. The battery had been removed and the tires were flat. A film of dust covered every part of it.

The cots, fan, and generator were a different story. The generator wasn't new, but it appeared to be in good working order. Rhodes opened the gas tank. It wasn't full, but he could smell the gasoline inside it. The cots weren't new, either, but they'd been slept on recently. The fan looked as if it had come out of the box only a day or so ago; in fact, the empty blue-and-white box lay a few feet away, leaning against the cardboard boxes Rhodes had noticed earlier.

The top box in each stack was closed with packing tape. Rhodes took out his pocketknife and slit the tape right down the center of one of the boxes. Then he slit the tape where it overlapped the sides and flipped the top open.

Inside, there were three rows of quart mason jars. Rhodes folded his knife and slipped it back into his pocket. He didn't even have to take the jars out of the box to know what they contained.

He counted the boxes. Six to a stack, which meant thirty-six quarts to a stack. Even his elementary school homework was coming in handy these days. He could even multiply thirty-six times three in his head and come out with 108. If he was right, that is.

Even if he was wrong, there was a lot of whiskey there, far too much for anybody to sell in Blacklin County alone. Someone was moving into the high-end trade in the cities, or had already made the move.

Kergan must have been involved somehow, since the bootleggers were using his shed, though possibly they'd started doing that only since he'd moved away. Maybe he hadn't known what was going on, though that seemed unlikely.

Now Rhodes had another decision to make. It was too bad that Mellon wasn't around to help him.

Rhodes didn't know who owned the still or the whiskey. He didn't know who'd made the whiskey, either, though he thought it must have been Rapper and Nellie. Somehow or other, the two of them were connected to the Crawfords.

Rhodes had to decide what to do. He could break up the still and the whiskey bottles, or he could wait around and see who came back to the shed.

Or he could do both.

Or neither.

He could hide in the shed and wait for Rapper and Nellie to return, or he could come back some other time and try to catch them there.

Once again, he found that he didn't like either of the choices he was offering himself.

How likely was he to catch them if he came back later? If they realized that someone had been in the shed, they'd load up, leave, and never come back. Rhodes didn't think he'd left any sign of his presence, but he couldn't afford to take the chance that he had.

If he hid inside and waited, he couldn't use the generator and the fan. Rapper and Nellie would hear the noise. And without the fan, Rhodes wouldn't be able to stay there more than a half hour or so, not with the door closed. It was close and stuffy enough even with it open. Rhodes thought that if he touched the west wall of the building, he might burn his hand.

Even if he waited, he couldn't be sure they'd come back that afternoon or even that night. He might just be wasting his time. He could call Hack and have someone else stake the place out, keep a twenty-four-hour watch on it. That might be the best thing to do, though it wasn't a very cost-effective use of personnel. He didn't have enough deputies to cover the county even when they were all on patrol.

Something else occurred to him. What if Rapper and Nellie weren't the ones staying there at all? He didn't have any proof that they were, just a strong suspicion. The only evidence was a scanty description provided by Seepy Benton.

Rhodes went out and closed the door of the shed. He looked at the house. He could wait there for a while. Even if the electricity was turned off and there was no air-conditioning, the house was bound to be cooler than the shed if he opened some windows. He'd have to be careful about that. He didn't want anyone coming along to notice the open windows and realize that someone was in the house.

He'd have to hide the car, too. He could park it behind the shed, where it would be out of sight of the road.

Just as he started toward the car, he saw a cloud of dust on the road. As he watched, a black pickup came around the curve.

Well, he thought, at least I won't have to worry about opening those windows.

TWENTY-TWO

THE DRIVER OF THE PICKUP didn't try to run Rhodes down this time. He just kept right on going, passing by the house and sending dust rolling Rhodes's way.

Rhodes was in the county car and after the pickup in seconds. The county road wasn't graveled, and the dust flying up behind the pickup, along with the dark windows, made it impossible for Rhodes to see who was driving or even if there was a passenger. He just assumed that Rapper and Nellie were inside the cab. He got as close as he could to them while trying to keep the car on the narrow road and out of the ditches.

He also called Hack and told him to send some backup.

"Where you want me to send it?" Hack asked.

It was a good question. All Rhodes lacked was a good answer. He looked out the window and, peering through the dust, saw the gravestones and oak trees of the Plunkett Cemetery. He told Hack where he was.

"That road's got more'n a couple of others that connect up to it," Hack said. "That truck you're chasin' could take any one of 'em."

Rhodes tried to get the county's geography straight in his head.

"This road comes out on the county road that goes past Louetta Kennedy's store, doesn't it?"

"Louetta's dead. Store's closed."

"You know what I mean."

"You don't have to get irritable." Hack paused. "Yeah, if you keep on goin', you'll come out about a half mile up the road from Louetta's old place. Turn right, you'll go past the store and wind up in the Big Woods. Turn left, you'll go back to Thurston."

Rhodes didn't think Rapper and Nellie would be going back to Thurston.

"Send somebody to the Big Woods," he said, and signed off.

It made sense that Rapper and Nellie would head for the woods. In fact, if they were making whiskey, the woods would be a good place for them to do it. It was a good bet that they could find a place there where they wouldn't be bothered by passersby.

The Big Woods was a throwback to earlier times. The trees had never been cut, and the place was like the famous Big Thicket in deep East Texas, only smaller. It was the kind of place where feral pigs took shelter from hunters. Rhodes sometimes thought an ivory-billed woodpecker might be hiding in there, though no one had ever searched for one.

Rhodes remembered yet another snippet of a poem from his high school days. It wasn't one that he'd had to memorize, but somehow a line had stuck in his mind. He hadn't thought of it in years, something about a woods that was "lovely, dark and deep." The Big Woods qualified on the last two counts, but as far as Rhodes was concerned, there wasn't anything lovely about them. The poem had also involved snow, Rhodes recalled, but there wasn't likely to be any of that, either.

Rhodes had had experiences in the Big Woods before, and those experiences hadn't been good ones. Far from it. One of them had started out all right, with the discovery of some mammoth bones, but it had all been downhill from there. Before it was over, Rhodes had tangled with things like snakes, wild hogs, and murderers. Rapper was as bad as any of those things, and a little worse than a couple of them, at least in Rhodes's estimation.

The county car hit a rut and bounced so hard that Rhodes's

head almost hit the roof. He jerked the wheel to keep the car going straight and told himself not to let his mind wander if he hoped to get to the woods in one piece.

It didn't take long to get there, no more than ten minutes. The pickup slowed and made the turn toward the woods, picking up speed on the better road. Rhodes stayed right behind. He hadn't turned on the light bar and siren earlier, but he did now. He didn't think the lights and noise would slow Rapper down or even give him a second thought, but it might serve as a warning to any cars they might meet.

They roared past Louetta Kennedy's store and past the place where the mammoth bones had been found on the bank of a creek. The bones had created a little excitement in the beginning, but in the end nothing had ever come of the find. Most of the bones had proved too brittle to preserve, and the creek had flooded, making removing them too difficult.

That had been a few years earlier. Rhodes wished the creek would flood again, and soon.

The road didn't go into the woods. It curved off and bypassed them, but Rapper didn't seem to know that. He wasn't slowing down for the curve.

Rhodes soon saw why. Rapper was going into the woods, and he was going to drive there. The pickup went off the road and down the bank of the creek, rocking from side to side. Rhodes thought it might flip over, but it didn't. It hit the creek bed hard, bottomed out, and rebounded, throwing up a little water from the trickle that was there. Then, with its tires chewing dirt and dead grass and throwing them out behind, it climbed the opposite bank.

Rhodes wasn't sure the county car was built to take the punishment the truck could, but it was too late for him to do anything but give it a try. He careened into the ditch, bouncing around like a rubber ball. When the car hit the creek bed, it almost stalled out, but Rhodes somehow gave it a jolt of gas at just the right time and it shot forward. For a second, Rhodes thought the car was going to stick nose-first into the bank, and he actually pulled back on the wheel. His arms strained and the tendons stood out in his neck. It was as if he believed he could lift the front end of the car up by his own power. Maybe he succeeded, because the hood bounced up, the back tires caught, and the car plowed up the bank.

Rhodes saw that Rapper wasn't going to stop at the tree line. With the big brush guard on the truck, he wouldn't have to. He could sweep past the smaller trees and even run over some of them.

Rhodes, however, could not. There were just some things the county car couldn't stand up to. Rapper might blaze a trail, but it wouldn't do for Rhodes to try to follow it. He was going to have to go after Rapper on foot.

The pickup crashed into the trees and went right on, but Rhodes stopped his car and got out. He unlocked the shotgun from the rack and looked into the trees where the pickup had disappeared.

Rhodes remembered three things. One was the last time he'd chased Rapper into some woods. That hadn't worked out too well for Rapper, but it had been a close call for Rhodes, as well. That was one thing.

The second had happened not long after the mammoth bones had been discovered by a man named Bud Turley. Rhodes had followed Turley into these same woods. Turley had left in even worse shape than Rapper had been in when Rhodes had finished with him. In Turley's case, however, Rhodes hadn't done the major part of the damage. A snake had.

The third time had been the earliest, and Rhodes had suffered an unfortunate encounter with some feral hogs. He'd wound up in the hospital himself that time, and he'd never felt the same about bacon since.

Rhodes didn't want to go through any of those things again,

and he certainly didn't want to wind up with a copperhead snake hanging from some part of his anatomy. He disliked snakes even more than he disliked feral hogs.

What worried him almost as much as the possibility of encountering snakes and hogs was that Rapper was smarter than Turley, and Rapper had company. Nellie, while not exactly a mental giant, tipped the odds in Rapper's favor.

Rhodes knew that waiting for backup would be the smart thing. He also knew that if he waited too long, Rapper might smash his way right through the Big Woods and out the other side, or just abandon the truck and run for it, after which he'd disappear again, maybe for a few years, maybe forever. Rhodes really wanted to get him this time.

So he started walking into the woods. It appeared that Rapper had followed a rough path that he already knew was there. Rhodes realized he might have been able to get the county car in after all, but he didn't think it would be a good idea to try. He'd just slip along quietly and see where the trail led him. He thought he could guess.

After he'd gone about twenty yards, he stopped to listen. If Rapper was still driving, the pickup should have been making plenty of noise, but an odd silence hung over the woods. Rapper's truck must have stopped after reaching some destination or running into a tree. Rhodes figured it was the former, even though he wished it could be the latter. Whatever had happened, the noise of the truck crashing along had scared even the squirrels and birds into silence for the time being.

It was late afternoon, and the sun was going down. It wouldn't be dark for a while, but where Rhodes was, the shadows were deepening. The farther into the trees he went, the darker it would be.

Again he thought about waiting, but if Rapper got away, he'd never forgive himself. He kept moving forward.

The mistake he'd made was a simple one. He told himself that anybody could have made it, but he knew that wasn't true. Rapper had outsmarted him again, which he realized as soon as Nellie stepped out behind him, stuck a pistol in his back, and said, "Hey, Sheriff. Long time no see."

Nellie had a high opinion of his wit. Rhodes didn't.

"Is that a shotgun in your hands," Nellie said, "or are you just glad to see me?"

Rhodes didn't answer. He was too busy chewing himself out for letting Rapper get the better of him. Obviously, he'd let Nellie out of the truck and kept on going. Rhodes imagined he'd said something like "That dumbass sheriff'll be concentrating on the truck. He won't expect you to be laying for him. Hide behind a tree and you can get the drop on him."

And that's what Nellie had done. The Indian Head penny hadn't helped a bit.

"I guess it's a shotgun," Nellie said. "I guess you aren't glad to see me, either."

"I'm not," Rhodes said.

He supposed he should have derived a little satisfaction from having been right about who was in the pickup, but somehow it just wasn't a satisfying situation.

"Rapper said you wouldn't be. You just put the shotgun down now. Don't drop it. Lay it down real easy."

Rhodes didn't have much choice. He could have tried to spin around and shoot Nellie, but Nellie wasn't so slow that he wouldn't shoot first. And probably second, too. Rhodes put the gun on the ground and straightened back up.

"Walk on a couple of steps and then stop," Nellie said.

When Rhodes had done that, Nellie picked up the shotgun and said, "This here's a lot better than the dinky little pistol I was carrying. I appreciate you bringing it along for me to use."

"You're welcome," Rhodes said. "That wouldn't be a twenty-five-caliber pistol you're carrying, would it?"

"What difference does it make?" Nellie said. "I got the shotgun now. I always did want to shoot somebody with one of these things just to see what'd happen to 'em. It's a twelve-gauge, ain't it?"

"What difference does that make?" Rhodes said.

Nellie gave a short laugh. "You're a really funny fella, Sheriff. I always did say that. Rapper, he never will go along with me. You might not believe this, but he don't like you a whole hell of a lot."

"I don't see why not."

"I bet you don't. Well, it's been nice to socialize with you and all like that, but now you better start walking. We got to go see Rapper. I hope he don't take this gun away from me. I've always wanted to shoot somebody with one."

"You said that already."

"Yeah, I guess I did. Just shows I mean it. Put your hands behind your neck and lace those fingers together."

Rhodes did as he was told. He was glad he didn't have any cuffs with him.

"That's the way to behave," Nellie said. "Now you can get moving."

Rhodes got moving.

TWENTY-THREE

RHODES DIDN'T BELIEVE Nellie would shoot him.

Nellie might be crazy, probably was, at least by Rhodes's standards, but Rapper wasn't. A criminal, yes, maybe even a killer, but a shrewd one. One who knew better than to kill a lawman. There wasn't a woods dark and deep enough to hide him and Nellie if they did that.

Nellie just followed along with Rapper for the most part, with Rapper doing the thinking for both of them. That was fine with Rhodes. He didn't want Nellie to try to think. He might sprain something in his brain and pull the trigger of the shotgun.

"Where are we going?" Rhodes asked.

Sweat ran down his temples. He couldn't feel the slightest touch of a breeze. The dying leaves hung on the trees as if frozen in place.

"You'll find out when we get there," Nellie said.

In less than a minute, they came to the black pickup. It was stopped in front of a big oak tree, but to Rhodes's disappointment, it hadn't hit the tree. The truck had just reached the end of the trail.

"Keep going," Nellie said, and Rhodes went around the truck and into the trees.

The shadows were thicker and darker there, and Rhodes could hardly see where he was going. When he mentioned that to Nellie, Nellie laughed.

"If you fall down, I'll see to it that you get up. Best you try to stay on your feet, though. Might be some snakes around here."

Rhodes knew more than he wanted to know about the snakes. He was careful not to get his feet tangled in some sticker-covered vine or to hit his head on a low-hanging limb.

"We got us a place a little farther along," Nellie said. "You'll see."

Rhodes could hardly wait. He wondered if whoever was going to back him up had arrived yet. If it was Ruth, she'd know enough to follow him, but would she be able to find her way through the woods? Rhodes hoped so.

He came to a place where the trees thinned out and he could see ahead more easily. The ground slanted down sharply into a hollow where there were hardly any trees at all. There was something else, however. In the center of the hollow was a still.

This still wasn't as small as the one now residing in the shed behind Kergan's house. It was a full-scale operation of shiny copper. Rhodes smelled the odor of the sour mash and the smoky scent of the burned oak that fired the boiler.

"Big 'un, ain't it?" Nellie said. "Big enough so we could throw you in there with the mash, give it a little flavor."

"Dr Pepper's better," Rhodes said. "So I've heard."

"That might not be bad," Nellie said. "What do you think, Rapper?"

"Might be too sweet," Rapper said.

"Yeah. So can we throw the sheriff in?"

"Throw him in the fire instead," Rapper said, stepping out from behind the still. "Burn him. Be the best thing to do, don't you think, Sheriff?"

Rapper hadn't been named for his ability to bust a rhyme. He'd been around for a lot longer than the Hip-Hop Nation. His gray hair was thin, and he slicked it back on the top and sides to reveal a sharp widow's peak. Rhodes noticed that he'd added a little ponytail in back, if you could call it that. It was so short that it didn't seem to qualify.

If his hair hadn't been so thin, he might have been able to grow it longer and cover up the mangled ear, or what was left of it. It hadn't improved any since Rhodes had shot most of it off, and Rapper wasn't trying to hide it.

He waggled his fingers at Rhodes to show they weren't all there, either.

"Remember me, Sheriff?" he said.

"How could I forget?"

Rapper grinned. He was no taller than when Rhodes had last seen him, but his belly had gotten bigger. It wasn't flabby, though. It looked hard enough to stop a bullet.

"You owe me, Sheriff," Rapper said. "You owe me big-time."

"You wouldn't want to hurt me, Rapper. It would cause you too much trouble."

"You never can tell," Rapper said. "Anyway, I think I'm in plenty of trouble already if you leave here. Maybe we could arrange for you to die in some kind of accident. An exploding boiler, maybe."

"You're pretty good at arranging accidents and explosions, aren't you?"

"I don't know what you're talking about. But blowing up the still would be a waste of good copper. We can't have that. Throw me that shotgun, Nellie."

The shotgun sailed past Rhodes. Rapper snatched it out of the air and pointed it at Rhodes.

"I always wanted to see somebody shot with one of those things," Nellie said.

Rhodes wished he'd stop saying that.

"But not me," Nellie said, stepping around Rhodes and staying well away from him. "The way that buckshot spreads, I might get hit, too."

Nellie didn't look much different from the last time Rhodes had seen him, except that he appeared to have stopped dyeing his hair, which was now pretty solidly gray. Whatever he had used on it before had given it an odd greenish tint, and Rhodes wondered if that was why he'd given up the dye.

"How are the ribs, Nellie?" Rhodes asked.

"Shoot him, Rapper," Nellie said. "Splatter him a little bit."

"Wouldn't be prudent at this time," Rapper said in a fair imitation of David Spade imitating the first George Bush.

Rhodes thought Rapper had a better sense of humor than Nellie, but not by much.

"Well, then, we oughta burn him up, like you said. Or throw him in the mash."

"We don't want anybody getting sick from drinking our wares," Rapper said. "That wouldn't do our business any good."

"He's gonna ruin our business anyway. We should've started up in some other county. He's always getting in our way."

Rhodes thought the same thing. It seemed like bad planning on Rapper's part to come back to a place where he'd had so much trouble in the past. He could understand the still, though. They could make money with it, and it wasn't nearly as risky as a meth lab.

"You know why we came here, Nellie," Rapper said. "But it looks like we'll have to be leaving now, and that's too bad. We had things set up pretty nice."

"If you're not gonna kill him," Nellie said, his disappointment evident in the tone of his voice, "what're you gonna do with him?"

"I don't quite have that figured out yet."

"Can we at least hurt him a little?"

Rhodes had never liked Nellie much. He was liking him less with every passing second.

"I'm going to put my hands down," he said.

His shoulder hurt, and he was tired of standing there like a prisoner, even if he was one. He didn't wait for Rapper's response. He just lowered his arms to his sides.

"I guess that's all right," Rapper said.

Nellie twitched. He shifted his weight from one foot to the other, swinging his body in time to some tune Rhodes couldn't hear.

"Better watch him, Rapper," Nellie said. "He's sneaky."

"Yeah. We'd better tie him up while we decide what to do about him. Get some rope."

Nellie stuck his pistol in the waistband of his worn jeans and walked over to a small stack of oak barrels. A piece of rope lay on top of one of them.

"Think this is long enough?" he said, holding it up.

"It'll do," Rapper told him. "Sheriff, you go sit down by that tree over there." He pointed the barrel of the shotgun at a young hackberry tree with a trunk about six inches in diameter. "You slide down the trunk real slow, with your hands behind you and your wrists crossed. Nellie, you tie his hands together when he sits down."

Rhodes went over to the tree and turned so his back was scraping the trunk. He wondered where his backup was. He remembered that the last time Ruth had come out this way to help him, she'd gotten lost. It could have happened again. She might be wandering around in the woods, looking for him. Or maybe her wrist was bothering her and she couldn't drive so well.

For whatever reason, she wasn't on the scene now, and Rhodes was worried that if she didn't come soon, he'd be beyond needing her help. Even if Rapper didn't kill him, he'd get away clean again, and Rhodes wanted to prevent that.

He supposed that in the absence of backup he'd have to help himself, so it was a good thing that Rapper and Nellie had made it easier for him.

Because Rhodes had been carrying the shotgun and because he didn't have a sidearm in plain sight, Nellie, who wasn't exactly the sharpest tack in the box, must have assumed he wasn't carrying another weapon. Rapper, on the other hand, must have figured that Nellie would have checked.

For once, Rhodes was glad he'd been using the ankle holster. If he'd been wearing a conventional rig, even Nellie couldn't have missed it.

The trick would be getting to the pistol before Rapper could cut him in half with the twelve-gauge. Rhodes knew it wouldn't be easy.

Then Nellie helped him out again. Instead of walking wide and circling around behind the tree, Nellie walked straight toward Rhodes. He was going to pass right in front of Rapper for a split second.

"Watch it!" Rapper said, realizing too late what was about to happen.

"What?" Nellie said, turning to face him.

Rhodes flung himself to the side, hit the ground, and rolled over twice. His shoulder twinged painfully, but he hardly noticed.

The shotgun boomed, and buckshot ripped leaves and limbs off the trees just above Rhodes and to his right. He pulled his knee up to his chest, causing his pants leg to rise high enough for him to get his fingers on the pistol grips.

He ripped the .38 free and fired off a round from where he lay, not thinking he'd hit anything, but hoping to confuse Rapper.

The sound of his shot was drowned out by another blast from the twelve-gauge, and Rhodes felt some of the buckshot rip through his shirt and scrape his side.

He raised his head a couple of inches and fired again. He didn't hit Rapper. He heard the slug hit the copper boiler with a metallic twang.

Nellie was on the run, but he didn't have the shotgun. Rhodes would worry about him later. He rolled to his left, raised up, saw Rapper turn the shotgun toward him.

Rhodes pulled the trigger of the .38. Rapper yelled and the

shotgun went flying. Rapper sat down hard. It looked to Rhodes as if one of his hands was gone.

Nellie had disappeared. Rhodes scrambled to his feet, but he was only halfway off the ground when something like the world's biggest hammer hit him in the head.

After that, he didn't know what happened for a while.

TWENTY-FOUR

"I THOUGHT MAYBE they'd killed you," Ruth Grady said.

Rhodes was propped against the hackberry tree where Nellie was supposed to have tied him. His head throbbed, and when he put his hand to his head, he felt a tender knot about the size of a hen's egg.

"Maybe they did," he said.

"I don't think so. You might have a concussion, though. Do you think you can walk?"

Rhodes wasn't sure he could even stand up.

"Give me a minute," he said. "What did I get hit with?"

"I don't see anything," Ruth said.

Nellie's pistol, then, Rhodes thought, wishing he had thicker hair or could stand to wear a hat. Either one might have helped. He thought about Sage Barton. Nothing like this had happened to him in the book. Rhodes had a feeling that nothing like this ever would. Sage Barton was too smart to get outwitted by a couple of guys like Rapper and Nellie.

He turned his head so he could see the still. It hadn't gone anywhere, and there was only one of it. That's a good sign, he thought. He could see Ruth clearly, too. She was standing over him with a concerned look.

"I'll be all right," he said.

"There's blood on your shirt," Ruth pointed out.

Rhodes pulled his shirt up and had a look. "Just a scratch. How's your wrist?"

"It's fine. Don't worry about me. You're the one who was unconscious."

"Just a little bump. Did you see what happened?"

Ruth shook her head. "I didn't see any of it. All I know is that I found your car and was about to follow a track into the woods, when I heard shots. I wasn't sure where they were coming from. A couple of minutes later, I heard a car start, and the next thing I knew, that black truck was coming at me again. In reverse, this time. I barely had time to get out of the way. I thought I'd better look around and see if you were all right. You weren't. That's about it."

"That was Rapper and Nellie in the truck. You remember them?"

"I remember. They're back?"

"They're back. That's their still over there."

"It's a lot bigger than the other one."

"Yeah. They stole that one and moved it to Jerry Kergan's place in Thurston. I followed them here from there. They've been making and selling a lot of 'shine. Hauling in water, I guess, since the creek's about dry. They could do that here and nobody would see them." Rhodes paused. Mentioning the water had made him thirsty. He could have used a drink. "I let them get the best of me again. Rapper's hurt, though, maybe bad enough that he'll need some help. Am I making sense?"

"I think so."

"I must be okay, then."

Rhodes got to his feet. He was a little dizzy at first, but the feeling passed quickly. He looked around and saw his pistol lying nearby. The shotgun wasn't far from where Rapper had been standing.

Rhodes told Ruth to check the shotgun. While she was doing that, he bent over to pick up the .38. He was hardly dizzy at all when he straightened up, but instead of putting the pistol back in the ankle holster, he stuck it in his waistband. No need to bend if he didn't have to.

"This twelve-gauge is messed up," Ruth said, holding it by the end of the barrel.

The stock was splintered and had blood on it.

"Bag it," Rhodes said. "If we ever need Rapper's DNA, we'll have it."

"I don't have a bag with me."

"There's one in the car. We need to get to Jerry Kergan's place."

"Why?"

"That's where Rapper will be going, if he's able. There's a lot of whiskey there. He won't want to leave it."

"He's losing blood," Ruth said. "I saw more on the ground where the gun was."

"If those feral hogs that bed up in here smell it, we might have company before long."

Having had a run-in with the hogs once before, Rhodes didn't want to meet them again.

Neither did Ruth. "Let's get out of here, then."

Rhodes started walking. "Rapper won't get help unless he's desperate. Let's see if we can get to that whiskey before it's gone."

"I'm right behind you," Ruth said, and she followed him into the trees.

"Be careful," Rhodes told her. It didn't get dark until nine o'clock or so at that time of year, but even at twilight it was hard to see in the trees. "You don't want to step on a snake."

"You're a real comfort, Sheriff. Are you sure your head's all right?"

Rhodes's head wasn't throbbing now. He just felt a dull ache in the place where Nellie had hit him.

"It's fine. I'll be able to drive."

When they got to the cars, however, he saw that he wouldn't be doing any driving.

"I thought maybe I heard a crash," Ruth said as they looked at Rhodes's county car. "Rapper must really hate you."

"You could be right," Rhodes said.

Rapper and Nellie had wanted to get away fast, so they hadn't done any more to Rhodes than Nellie had already accomplished. Maybe they thought he was dead, or hoped he was. But they couldn't just leave without lashing out in some way or another. That wouldn't be like Rapper. So they'd plowed into the side of the car with the brush guard of the truck. Rhodes thought they might have hit it more than once.

"I can't wait to tell the commissioners about this," he said.

"We're heavily insured," Ruth said. "They won't mind."

"You don't know them very well, do you?"

"No, and I don't think I want to. Come on. I'll get out the first-aid kit and we'll put something on your side and your head."

Ruth went to her own cruiser and opened the trunk. She bagged the shotgun and got out the first-aid kit. Rhodes wanted to get started, but Ruth was adamant about doing something to his wounds. The antiseptic she used stung, but Rhodes hardly noticed. He helped her stick a bandage on his side, but he wouldn't let her do anything to his head. He started to get into the car as Ruth put away the first-aid kit.

"I'll drive," she told him.

Rhodes got in on the passenger side and called Hack to tell him to send a wrecker for the other cruiser.

"He might not be able to find it," Hack said. "Off down there in the woods like that."

"It's not in the woods," Rhodes said. "It's at the edge of the woods. He can see it from the road if he looks."

"I'll tell him, but I can't promise anything."

Rhodes said that was good enough and asked if a deputy was near Thurston.

"Just Ruth, and you know where she is."

Rhodes had figured that was the case. "Get the word out to the DPS and the departments in all the surrounding counties. Tell them to be looking for a black Dodge pickup, no license plates. It's Rapper and Nellie."

"Those two never learn."

Rhodes thought about the knot on his head. He might be the one who never learned.

"Call Jack Mellon, too. He'll need to come up tomorrow and have a look at the still."

"I'll call him as soon as I call the other counties."

"Check with all the hospitals while you're at it," Rhodes said. "Rapper might be hurt enough to check into an ER."

"How'd you hurt him?"

"Shot him in the hand."

"Just like the Lone Ranger."

"Not quite. He and Nellie probably killed Jerry Kergan and Terry Crawford," he said. "We need to find them before they lose themselves somewhere."

"I'll put out the word," Hack said. "They never seem to get caught, though."

"We'll get them this time," Rhodes said, but even he didn't believe it.

THEY GOT TO Kergan's house too late. The still was in the shed, but the whiskey was gone.

"Rapper must not have been hurt as much as you thought," Ruth said. "Not if they loaded all that whiskey."

"There were only eighteen boxes," Rhodes said. "Nellie could have loaded them by himself if Rapper told him to."

"Somebody will catch them, a state trooper or somebody."

"Right," Rhodes said.

"It could happen."

"Right," Rhodes said again.

IVY WAS CONCERNED about Rhodes's head.

"I think you should go to the ER and have it looked at," she said. "You might have a concussion."

Rhodes suspected that she'd been talking to Ruth. "I don't have a concussion. I'm fine."

"You always say that."

She was right. Rhodes always made light of things that happened to him. All the same, he was convinced that he just had a knot on his head and nothing more.

Unless you counted his chest, which was quite colorful now, and his shoulder which still hurt if he moved his arm much, and the place where the shot had grazed him.

"What about that place on your side?" Ivy asked. She hadn't overlooked it, as Rhodes had hoped she might. He should have known better. "What's that bandage covering up?"

"Just a scratch," Rhodes said. "Ruth put some antiseptic on it. It doesn't even hurt."

"I'm sure. When's the last time you had a tetanus shot?"

"It's only been a year or so."

Ivy shook her head. "I hope you hurt Rapper as much as he hurt you."

"I did."

Rhodes wasn't sure even of that, but considering the blood on the shotgun stock, he figured that Rapper had lost a good portion of his hand. Maybe the fingers, maybe just the meaty part of the palm. Rhodes wondered if it was the same hand that had already been maimed a little.

"I thought the book signing went well this afternoon," he said, hoping to distract Ivy.

It worked.

"I wish I could have gotten there sooner and stayed a little longer," she said. "That was quite a crowd. Did anybody take pictures?"

Rhodes wasn't sure. "Jennifer Loam was there. She took a couple, I think."

"I'll have to get a few extra copies of the paper tomorrow if there's a picture."

"I won't be in it," Rhodes said. "Claudia and Jan wrote the book, not me."

"Everybody in Clearview knows there wouldn't be a Sage Barton if it weren't for you."

"Sage Barton wouldn't have as much trouble with Rapper as I do. He'd have put Rapper away long ago."

"I'm not worried about Rapper. You'll get him this time for sure."

"Right," Rhodes said.

TWENTY-FIVE

THE NEXT MORNING after he fed the dogs and the cat, Rhodes went to the jail in the county car he'd borrowed. It wasn't as new as the one he was used to driving, but it would do. He suspected he'd be getting an even newer one soon, because there wasn't going to be much anybody could do about the one Rapper had wrecked.

Considering that, Rhodes hoped Hack might have some good news for him, but of course there wasn't any.

"No word from any DPS troopers about the truck," Hack said. "No word from any hospitals about a man with a wounded hand. No sign of Nellie or Rapper anywhere. Looks like they've dropped off the face of the earth."

He didn't add the word *again,* but he didn't have to. Rhodes knew it was implied.

Hack paused and glanced at Lawton, who just grinned.

"That ain't all," Hack said.

Rhodes sighed. "Tell me."

"We found out who owned the donkey."

"It coulda been a mule," Lawton said. "Mules are a lot more common around here. You see 'em ever' now and then. Turned out it was a donkey, though."

"Who was the owner?" Rhodes asked, hoping to stave off another discussion of the differences between mules and donkeys.

"Pete Langston. You know him?"

"Lives on Peach Street?"

"That's the one. He's got himself a little pasture just out of town, not anything on it but some mesquite trees and a little barn. That's where he had the donkey. He bought it for his kids to ride."

"How'd it get out?"

"He says it didn't. He says it was stolen. He called and asked if it was still the law that a man could shoot somebody who stole his donkey."

"Still the law?"

"He said a donkey was the same as a horse," Lawton said. "Said it was the law that you could shoot horse thieves, so couldn't you shoot a donkey thief?"

Hack looked as if he might shoot Lawton for breaking into his explanation.

"I blame cable TV," Lawton went on, ignoring Hack's angry frown. "People watchin' all those old Westerns. They think we're still back in the Wild West days."

Rhodes didn't want to get into that discussion, either.

"So what did you tell Mr. Langston?" he asked Hack.

Hack looked pleased to have the floor again. "I told him if that was ever the law, and I wasn't sure that it was, it's not the law now and he'd better not go shootin' anybody."

"Who did he want to shoot?"

"Franklin Anderson."

Rhodes must have looked dumbfounded, because Lawton and Hack both had a good laugh at his expression.

"Why Anderson?" Rhodes asked when he could get their attention again.

"'Cause somebody told him that they saw Anderson with a donkey in his trailer, and he naturally assumed Anderson was the one that stole his donkey."

"Naturally," Rhodes said. "I hope you straightened him out."

"I did. Told him he'd have to pay to get his donkey back,

too. He didn't like that one little bit. Said he's a taxpayer, and it was the county's job to round up strays."

"Did you remind him that his taxes would be even higher if we had to bill all the taxpayers for the care and feeding of stray donkeys?"

"Sure did. He didn't want to hear it, though."

"Did you tell him to check his fence?"

"Yep. That made him even madder. So I told him that he'd have to pay up ever' time we caught that donkey out at the car wash."

"How'd he take that?"

"He said if he saw who was lettin' his donkey out, he'd shoot him, 'cause that was the law."

"I think you oughta go to his place and disconnect his cable, Sheriff," Lawton said. "Or just tell him he can't subscribe to that Western channel."

"He might have a satellite dish 'stead of the cable," Hack said. "Lots of folks got those now."

Rhodes wasn't interested in getting into that. He said, "Send Buddy by to have a talk with him. I'm going to see Mel Muller about our departmental Web site."

"What about Rapper?"

"If any news comes in, you can get in touch with me."

Rhodes started for the door, but Hack didn't let him get there.

"I called the TABC," Hack said. "Mellon's coming back this afternoon around two. You gonna be here?"

"I'll try to be. If I'm not, have Ruth take him to the still. She can find it."

"What if Rapper's around?"

"He won't be."

"One more thing, then," Hack said. "That Benton fella called late yesterday."

Rhodes turned around. "What did he want?"

"It was something about those possums in Miz Owens's

attic. He wants to talk to you about that. He said he'd be out at the college this mornin' if you wanted to drop by."

Rhodes didn't want to drop by, but he would if he had a chance. He was curious to see what Benton had to say about the possums.

"Is that about it?" Rhodes said. "No other calls, nobody else wants to shoot somebody? No bank robberies?"

"That's it," Hack said. "You can go now."

"Thanks," Rhodes said. "I appreciate it."

MEL MULLER OPENED her door when Rhodes knocked. She wore a gray sweatshirt and red sweatpants. Working at home has its advantages, Rhodes thought.

"What?" she said. "Is this about that Web site again? I told you it takes a long time to do a quality job. I'm working on it."

"I know you are. So does Commissioner Burns, but I want him to hear it from you. I don't like being a go-between."

"I don't want to talk to him."

Rhodes didn't believe her. One thing he'd decided when he was trying to sleep the previous night was that she and Burns didn't have anything to do with the whiskey and the stills or the death of Jerry Kergan. They just had a problem with stubbornness.

Mel had told Rhodes more than once that Burns should come by himself or call her himself, but Burns wasn't going to do that. Rhodes figured he was intimidated by Muller because he'd treated her badly, and now he didn't want to face her. So Rhodes was going to put them together and let them work out their differences. Then maybe Burns would leave him alone about the Web site. And who could tell. It was possible that they'd reach an accommodation. Burns might even ask her for a date.

"I think you'd better come along with me, whether you want to talk to him or not," Rhodes said.

"Are you going to arrest me?"

"No. Just taking you for a ride."

"You sound like somebody in a Mafia movie."

Rhodes had been hoping he sounded like Edward G. Robinson. Maybe Mel was too young to remember him.

"I'll get ready," she said, giving in. "Come in and have a seat."

Rhodes went inside, and Mel disappeared. Rhodes shoved computer magazines off the chair. He wondered if they were the same ones he'd moved the last time he'd sat there.

It took her awhile, so he picked up one of the magazines and tried to read it. He discovered he could understand hardly any of it. He tossed the magazine back on the floor.

When Mel returned, she had changed clothes and put on makeup.

Suspicions confirmed, Rhodes thought. When it comes to shrewd intuition, Sage Barton has nothing on me. For that matter, neither does Dr. Phil.

They drove to the precinct barn, and Mrs. Wilkie greeted them when they came in. Rhodes explained why they were there, and she allowed them to go into Burns's office without being announced.

Burns was surprised to see them, and he stammered a little in his confusion. Rhodes let him suffer for a few seconds and then said, "I want you two to talk over the Web site design and get things settled. You can take Ms. Muller home when you're finished, can't you?"

"I, well, I guess I can, but that's, uh, county time. I have things to do, and—"

"And you can't cheat the taxpayers," Rhodes said, finishing the sentence for him. "I know that. Taking Ms. Muller home would be county business, related to the Web site she's working, just like bringing her here was."

"Yes, well, uh, I can see that. If it's all right with Ms. Muller, then, I guess we can talk."

"It's all right with her," Rhodes said. "Isn't it?"

Mel nodded.

"Good. I'll be talking to both of you later about the Web site."

Rhodes didn't give them a chance to say anything else. He left them there and drove to the community college building. Because of his experience with a mammoth dig a couple of years earlier, he'd visited one of the college instructors, Tom Vance, and knew where his office was located. He supposed Benton's office would be nearby, and it turned out to be only a few yards down the hallway.

Benton, however, wasn't there. A note taped to his door said that he was at Max Schwartz's music store. Rhodes hadn't noticed Benton's Saturn in the parking lot when he passed by the store, but he hadn't been looking for it. He'd had other things on his mind. Something had occurred to him, something he should have thought of before, and he realized he was going to have to talk to Mel Muller again. He could do that after he saw Benton, however, so he went back to his car and headed for the music store.

Benton's car was there all right. He must have been Schwartz's best customer. Maybe his only customer, since Schwartz's convertible was the only other car in the lot.

Rhodes parked beside the Saturn and went inside. A song Rhodes recognized was playing over the hidden speakers— "Tom Dooley" again.

Schwartz and Benton were talking at the counter in the back. Rhodes joined them.

"I was just telling Max about the possums you sent me to look for yesterday," Benton said. "Except there weren't any possums."

"Was it squirrels?" Rhodes said.

"No, it wasn't squirrels. It wasn't anything."

"Mrs. Owens said it was possums."

"That's because she wanted you to come out and look for them. It turned out that I was just as good. Maybe better."

Rhodes was confused, which wasn't an unusual condition for him when he was talking to Benton, who was getting more like Hack and Lawton every time Rhodes saw him.

"Just as good as what?" he said.

"As good as you."

"I never doubted that," Rhodes said. "But I'd like to know why Mrs. Owens felt that way."

"Her husband died a few years ago," Benton said. "She's lonesome."

"What does that have to do with possums?"

"I told you. There weren't any. I looked around up in the attic, but there was nothing up there and no sign of anything. Mrs. Owens just wanted somebody to talk to. That's why she called. She thought you'd be interesting because of the book."

"She was wrong," Rhodes said.

"Luckily, I had my guitar in the car," Benton went on. "I played her some songs, and she even sang along on 'Go Tell Aunt Rhody.'"

"That's a sad one," Schwartz said.

"I'll bet Deputy Grady would like it," Benton said, giving Rhodes a sideways look. "Especially the way I sing it."

"Maybe she would," Rhodes said. He wasn't going to play Dr. Phil for Benton. "I appreciate your helping out."

"I'm always happy to assist my local law enforcement."

"There's a right way and a wrong way to do that," Rhodes said, looking at Schwartz. "The wrong way would be to go after someone with a gun because they'd insulted your wife."

"I don't know what you're talking about," Schwartz said. "I didn't do anything like that."

"You thought about it, though."

"Look, those Crawfords are dangerous."

"One of them's not," Benton said. "He's dead."

"Yeah, but the other one's still around, and we're talking about when they both were. They were running some kind of a scam up there on that hill, even if they didn't have a meth lab. Somebody needed to do something."

"Somebody did do something," Rhodes said. "And now Terry's dead."

"I'm not saying that's a good thing."

"They won't be bothering Jackee anymore," Benton said. "They won't be selling whiskey, either."

"It's up to me to take care of that," Rhodes said. "Not citizens. I have to congratulate you about what you did for Mrs. Owens, though."

"You're welcome," Benton said.

"I hope you don't think I killed Terry Crawford," Schwartz said. "I couldn't do anything like that. And there's something else."

"What else?"

"Jackee and I have talked it over. We don't think it was Terry who bothered her that day. We're pretty sure it was Larry. They're hard to tell apart."

"It doesn't matter now. I don't think you killed Terry, and I have a pretty good idea who did." Schwartz relaxed a little, and Rhodes went on. "I do believe you wanted to make some kind of move against the Crawfords. It's a good thing you didn't. You might have been the one who got hurt."

Schwartz looked sheepish. "You're right. I did think about it. I wasn't going to do anything on my own, though. I was going to get some help. The trouble was, nobody wanted to help me."

"Good for them," Rhodes said.

"You don't have to worry about me," Benton said. "I promise I'll stick to helping widows with possum problems, or whatever comes up along those lines."

"Me, too," Schwartz said.

Rhodes nodded. "That's good, because I have something I want you to help me out with."

"We'll be glad to," Benton said, as if speaking for both of them. "What is it?"

"It has to do with flying saucers," Rhodes told them.

TWENTY-SIX

AFTER EXPLAINING ABOUT Dave Ellendorf, Rhodes used Schwartz's phone to call Burns's office. When Mrs. Wilkie answered, Rhodes said, "I'll be coming back by there to take Ms. Muller home."

"That might be a good idea," she said.

Rhodes didn't know what she meant, and he didn't get a chance to ask, because she'd already hung up.

"Is that Mel Muller you're talking about?" Benton said.

It wasn't any of his business, but Rhodes told him that it was. He added that she was building a Web site for the sheriff's department.

"I've heard that she does that kind of thing," Benton said. "So do I. It's just a sideline, but I'm really good at it. You should check out docbenton dot com sometime. It's a sample of what I can do."

"Maybe I'll do that," Rhodes said, though he didn't have any intention of following through.

"I'm pretty good with a computer," Benton said. "I teach math, but I've done a lot of work with databases and mathematical software."

If there was one thing Rhodes had no interest in, it was mathematical software, so he turned to Schwartz before Benton could elaborate.

"Do you think you can rig something up for Mr. Ellendorf?" Rhodes asked.

"Easy," Schwartz told him. "I have some old electrical components around here that'll make a good hum and buzz."

"Fine. The sooner you get it to Mr. Ellendorf, the better. Be sure to show him how to turn it on."

"What if it doesn't work?" Benton asked.

"It'll work," Rhodes said. "I guarantee it."

"No doubt about it," Schwartz said. "There won't be any more flying saucers in the neighborhood once my saucer repeller's on the job."

"That's what I thought," Rhodes said. "I knew that the academy would produce some graduates who'd do some good in this community."

"By repelling flying saucers?" Benton said.

"That, and by helping out with some other things. With possums, for example. You'll be going back to see Mrs. Owens, I hope."

"I said I'd drop by now and then. She likes my music. You could have Deputy Grady check on her, too."

Rhodes didn't mind playing Cupid for Mikey Burns, but he wasn't interested in getting involved in the love life of one of his deputies.

"You might want to talk to her yourself," Rhodes said. "I don't know if she likes guitar players."

"Some people don't," Schwartz said, as if he knew from experience.

"What about banjo players?" Benton said.

Schwartz shook his head. "Don't ask."

"MAYBE YOU SHOULD wait out here a few minutes," Mrs. Wilkie said when Rhodes got to the commissioner's office.

Rhodes thought she just wanted the pleasure of his company, until he heard the loud voices coming from behind the door to Burns's office.

Mrs. Wilkie looked worried. "They've been arguing for five minutes now."

"I'll see if I can settle them down," Rhodes said, and opened the door.

He was taken aback by what he saw. Mel Muller and Mikey Burns faced each other across Burns's desk, talking in angry tones. They broke off when Rhodes came in, and Mel turned to look at him. Neither she nor Burns looked glad he'd showed up.

"This is a private conversation, Sheriff," Burns said.

His tone made it clear that Rhodes could forget taking Dr. Phil's place anytime in the near future.

"I hope you're not arguing about that Web site," Rhodes said, though he knew that wasn't the problem.

Burns's voice was strained. "We're not arguing, and if we are, it's none of your business."

"I'm sure it's not, but I came to pick up Ms. Muller. I need her help with an investigation."

"What kind of investigation?" Muller asked, ignoring Burns and giving all her attention to Rhodes.

"Just a little computer work," Rhodes told her. "It might even have to do with a computer you're familiar with."

"Which computer would that be?" Burns asked.

Rhodes didn't think it would be a good idea to bring up Jerry Kergan's name at the moment.

"That's something I'll have to keep secret for now. Part of an ongoing investigation."

"If it's in my precinct, I have a right to know," Burns said.

"Not really," Rhodes replied. He was getting tired of Burns's act. "If you want to take it up with the ACLU, that's fine with me."

"You'd better not mess with me, Sheriff. I know about that car you destroyed last night."

Word gets around fast, Rhodes thought.

"I'm not messing with you, and what happened to the car

wasn't my fault. I'm sorry it happened, but that's just one of the hazards of enforcing the law."

"It's going to affect our insurance rates."

"That's too bad," Rhodes said. "Maybe we can make Rapper pay for it when we catch him."

"You'd better catch him, then, whoever he is," Burns said, though he and Rhodes both knew better than to think there'd be any restitution for the car.

Rhodes was tired of talking to Burns. He looked at Mel. "Would you be willing to help me out with that computer?"

She stood up. "As long as it gets me out of here. What do you want me to do?"

"You'll find out," Rhodes said. "I don't think you'll have any trouble."

"Good. Can we go now?"

"Sure."

She started out of the room, and Rhodes stepped aside to let her through the door.

Before Rhodes could leave, Burns said, "I'll talk to you later about your behavior, Sheriff."

"It's about time somebody did," Rhodes said.

"What does that mean?"

Rhodes didn't answer. He just closed the door. Mel wasn't in Mrs. Wilkie's office.

"She said she'd wait outside," Mrs. Wilkie said when Rhodes asked.

"Thanks. Could you make a phone call for me? I'm sure Mr. Burns wouldn't mind."

"I guess I can," Mrs. Wilkie said, and Rhodes asked her to look up the number for Schwartz's store.

"Call and tell him I'd like to speak to C. P. Benton, if he's there."

Mrs. Wilkie got the number and made the call. Benton was still at the store, and Rhodes took the phone to speak to him.

"Can you meet me at Dooley's in ten minutes?" Rhodes asked.

"I'm helping Max with the saucer repeller."

"He can handle that. I might need your computer skills."

"All right. I'm always glad to help out the law. That's why I was in the academy. I'll be there."

Rhodes handed the phone to Mrs. Wilkie, thanked her, and left.

MEL DIDN'T HAVE much to say at first. After Rhodes started the car and got under way, he asked if she was all right.

"I'm fine. Mikey Burns will never change. He's afraid to commit to anything."

By "anything," she means to her, Rhodes thought. He should have known that Burns wasn't going to reform instantly.

"Where are we going?" Mel asked.

"To Dooley's. You said you helped Jerry Kergan set up his accounting system, didn't you?"

"Not exactly. I showed him how, but I didn't really set things up for him."

"You could probably find the accounts on the computer, and if you did, you could print them out for me, though."

"Maybe. I can't be certain until I try."

"I have a lot of confidence in you," Rhodes said.

"Will this help you find out who killed Jerry?"

"I'm not sure. I hope so."

Because Kergan had been killed by Rapper, Rhodes was looking for a motive, and he suspected that the two had been dealing in bootleg whiskey. Kergan had already failed in the restaurant business once, and since the profit margin was so narrow even in a successful operation, Rhodes thought Kergan might have found a way to make enough money to keep him going until Dooley's started to turn a profit. If he had, there could be something in his records to show where the money had come from.

The problem with that theory was that Rapper hadn't been seen at the restaurant. Only the Crawfords had. So if Kergan had been doing business with anyone, it was more likely to have been Larry and Terry than Rapper.

In a way, that would be all right with Rhodes. He wanted to get Larry almost as much as he wanted to get Rapper.

Or maybe it was really Lawless he wanted to get. Lawless had recently represented a woman Rhodes had arrested for murder, and he'd almost gotten her off. In the process, Lawless had tried to cast Rhodes in a bad light, a villainous sheriff persecuting an innocent woman who couldn't possibly have done what he claimed she had.

After the trial, Rhodes told himself that Lawless had only been doing his job, and he'd told Lawless that he didn't hold any grudges. He'd been thinking almost the same thing when he'd talked to Judge Parry about Lawless and the academy.

It was easy to say that all was forgiven, and Rhodes believed he'd meant it. But maybe he hadn't. Maybe he was harboring a little resentment that he wasn't even aware of. At any rate, he'd like to beat Lawless again, and if Larry had been selling whiskey through Dooley's, it might be possible.

Benton's little Saturn was already at Dooley's, parked near the front door, when Rhodes and Mel arrived. The door had a strip of yellow-and-black crime-scene tape across it. Benton was standing beside his car, strumming a guitar.

"Who's that?" Mel asked.

"That's Dr. C. P. Benton. He teaches math at the college."

Mel looked skeptical. "He doesn't look like a math teacher."

"Don't let the guitar fool you. He's a math teacher all right, and a computer whiz besides."

Mel's skeptical expression didn't change as they got out of the car. Even hearing Benton's playing didn't change it.

Benton grinned at her and did his best to make her smile,

running through a few chords and singing a couple of lines of some song Rhodes didn't recognize.

Benton stopped playing and said, "Not a music lover?"

"Do you know 'Witch Doctor'?" Rhodes asked after he'd introduced them.

"No, but I know 'The Merry Minuet.'"

Benton plucked a few notes and sang something about rioting in Africa.

Mel smiled then. "That song's fifty years old," she said, "and nothing's changed."

Benton finished the song and put his guitar in a case in the backseat of his car. Mel stood by him, asking him computer questions that were more or less incomprehensible to Rhodes, who was feeling like a rival for Dr. Phil again.

"Let's go in and take a look at Kergan's computer," he said.

He went to the door and took down the crime-scene tape. He had a key, and he opened the door. They all entered the dark restaurant. Rhodes didn't know where the lights were located, but Benton did. He turned them on, and they went to Kergan's office.

"He needed a new computer," Benton said, looking at the box that sat on the floor by the workstation.

"He just used it for simple things," Mel said. "Nothing more complicated than a spreadsheet. He could have been using a Commodore sixty-four and he wouldn't have known the difference."

She and Benton had a little laugh at her comment. Rhodes didn't get the joke.

"Can you find his accounts?" he asked.

"I'm sure I can," Mel said.

"And if she can't find what you're looking for, I can," Benton said. "If it's there, I mean."

Mel looked at him. "Are you really any good?"

"I know quite a bit about computers. I even build Web sites. Check out docbenton dot com if you want to be impressed."

Rhodes had to admit that Benton didn't lack confidence in his abilities, whether he was talking about computers or musicianship.

Mel didn't say whether she wanted to be impressed by the Web site. She turned on the computer and waited for it to boot up.

"He didn't even use a password," she said after the computer had booted up.

She clicked on the mouse a few times, running through menus so fast that Rhodes didn't have a chance to get much of a look at them, not that he'd have known what they were even if he'd stared at them for a long time.

Benton watched, too. Rhodes detected a hint of admiration in his eyes. Ruth Grady might not be so interesting to him now, and Rhodes felt a little guilty about that. It was possible that Benton was just the guy for her. On the other hand, maybe he wasn't.

"Here's what you're looking for," Mel said, saving him from worry about his Dr. Phil-like maneuverings.

Rhodes looked at the computer monitor. Even he could tell that he was looking at the restaurant's regular accounts.

"What I want is something that would have been off the books," he said. "A record of dealing in something illegal. Whiskey sales."

"There's nothing like that here."

"Jerry didn't sell whiskey in the bar," Benton said. "I was here often enough. I would have known if he'd been doing something like that."

"He wouldn't do anything illegal," Mel agreed. "He wouldn't take that kind of chance."

"Just keep looking," Rhodes said.

Mel worked the mouse awhile longer. "Nothing," she said. "Jerry wasn't good enough at accounting to keep two sets of books anyway."

"Let me try," Benton said.

Mel got up, and Benton sat in the chair at the workstation.

"You won't find anything," Mel said.

"If it's here, I will."

And in only a couple of minutes, he did.

TWENTY-SEVEN

"HE PUT IT IN A FILE called 'Letters'?" Mel said. "Who'd ever look there?"

"Me," Benton said.

"Never mind," Rhodes said. "What does it tell you?"

"Not much," Benton said. "I'm not even sure it's what you think it is. It does seem to show that he took in some money, but it doesn't show that he paid any out. Wouldn't he have had to pay for whiskey if he bought it?"

"Of course," Mel said. "I knew he wasn't selling whiskey."

"I did, too," Benton said. "I told you that just a few minutes ago. Remember?"

Rhodes remembered, and he wished Kergan had made things a little more clear. According to what Rhodes could make out on the monitor screen, Kergan had recorded dates and amounts, but he hadn't said what the money was for. The amounts were for a hundred dollars or so at a time, but the times were pretty well separated. Maybe the money would have been enough to keep the restaurant going until business built up, or maybe not. Rhodes would have to go through the other accounts, or have someone do it for him, to be sure.

Unfortunately, there was no record of who'd given Kergan the money. For all Rhodes could prove, it might have fallen out of the sky.

"I'm going to leave you two with the computer," he said. "I

have to see a man about a still. If you can find out anything else about where that money came from, I'd appreciate it."

"We could take turns," Benton said to Mel. "Like a treasure hunt."

"I'll go first," she said.

"Can you give Mel a ride home?" Rhodes asked Benton.

"I'd be glad to."

Rhodes left them there, happy as a pair of scratch-off lotto winners.

JACK MELLON ARRIVED at the jail shortly after Rhodes got there, saving Rhodes from the grilling Hack and Lawton would have put him through about the morning's activities.

Rhodes drove Mellon down to the Big Woods. On the way, he told him about Rapper and Nellie.

"Sounds like they've been a real problem around here. Too bad they got away."

"We'll find them eventually," Rhodes said.

His side twinged, and he ran a hand over his chest. When he did that, his shoulder hurt. He owed Rapper a lot this time.

"If you don't find him, we will," Mellon said.

"Right," Rhodes replied.

RHODES PARKED at the edge of the woods, and they walked to the still. It was exactly as Rhodes and Ruth had left it. Rhodes had been sure Rapper wouldn't return for it. It was too big to dismantle easily, and Rapper wouldn't have been in any condition to do much work.

"Now that's what I call a still," Mellon said, looking it over with evident admiration. "I don't think I've ever seen one to equal it. How's it tie in with the little one you took me to see? The one that got lost?"

"I found that one again, too," Rhodes said. "It's in a barn not too far from here. I'll show it to you on the way back to town. The two fellas who were running this one stole it and hid it on someone's property."

Mellon walked around the still to get a good look at it.

"They must have been making enough whiskey to keep half the population of Dallas in illegal booze. I wonder who their contact was."

As soon as Mellon said those words, it came to Rhodes that he might know the contact's name.

"I think it was a man named Jerry Kergan. He was in the restaurant business here. He'd have known people in the same business in Dallas or Houston, maybe some places that would sell a little 'shine on the side. Kergan must have been helping Rapper and Nellie move the whiskey."

If Rhodes was right, that would explain the small amounts of money Kergan had received. He'd just been a go-between.

"We'll need proof of that before we can arrest him," Mellon said.

Mellon always wanted proof, but in this case, it didn't matter.

"His name was Jerry Kergan," Rhodes said. "He's dead."

He thought he knew now why Rapper had killed Kergan. Rapper must have known that Kergan went out for a smoke at about the same time every night, and seeing Rhodes in the parking lot, he might well have thought that Kergan had talked to him or considered talking to him. So he'd taken care of the perceived problem the way Rapper naturally would—by killing him.

"Can't arrest a dead man," Mellon said. "He must have made a ton of money before he died."

"Not really." Rhodes didn't mention that he'd seen the amounts. "I'm guessing, but I think he just set things up and didn't take part in any of the actual dealing."

"It would be hard to make a case against him, then, unless somebody ratted him out."

Rhodes didn't think Rapper and Nellie would ever inform on anybody. Not out of loyalty. They'd keep quiet just to be contrary, and Kergan was dead anyway.

Mellon banged a hand on the side of the still. "This baby would be able to put out a lot of liquor. It hasn't been used much, though."

"How can you tell?"

"Tell by looking. It hasn't been here long. I doubt more than three or four batches have been run through it."

The still did look new. Rhodes hadn't thought about that. The figures he'd seen of Kergan's accounts went back several months. Rapper hadn't been here that long. So Kergan hadn't been dealing with him. He must have been dealing with the Crawfords.

Then why had Rapper killed Kergan? Rhodes didn't have the answer after all.

"What do you want to do about the still?" he said.

"I want to get some pictures of it. Then we'll have our men come up here and dismantle it. We might as well pick up that other one you mentioned, too. What about the man who was running that one?"

"I haven't arrested him. It's like you said. I don't have any proof against him. He claims it was his brother's still, not his, and now he doesn't even have the still."

Mellon laughed. "Your job isn't any easier than mine. They don't pay us enough."

"Sad but true," Rhodes said.

BACK IN CLEARVIEW, Rhodes and Mellon stopped at McDonald's for a late lunch. Rhodes knew he shouldn't eat a Quarter Pounder, but he couldn't resist.

"You ever see that movie about the man who ate at McDonald's for a year or so?" Mellon said as they sat in the cruiser and unwrapped their burgers.

"No," Rhodes said, "and I don't want to."

"He didn't eat anything the whole time except for McDonald's food. He gained a lot of weight. Just about ruined his health."

"Don't tell me any more," Rhodes said, taking a satisfying bite of his burger.

IT WAS AS IF Rapper and Nellie had disappeared into some alternate universe. No reports came in about the black Dodge, and there were no reports from any hospitals about treating a man with a gunshot wound to his hand.

"Those two gotta be somewhere," Hack said when he told Rhodes the news. "They can't just disappear like Houdini."

"Looks like they can," Lawton said. "Looks like they have. They've sure done it before. Might's well write this one off and put it in the *unsolved* file."

Rhodes wasn't going to do that. "I want a deputy to drive by that spot of woods where Rapper had the still every half hour tonight. Rapper might sneak back if his hand's better."

"That's gonna leave a lot of the county unpatrolled," Hack said.

"Can't be helped. Besides, if the deputy cruises through Thurston often enough, it'll make Hod Barrett happy."

"Wouldn't anything make Hod happy," Lawton said.

Rhodes thought Lawton was right. "Well, whatever happens, it's just for one night. Mellon's crew will get the still tomorrow. They'll take the little one, too."

"You want the deputy to watch Kergan's barn tonight?"

"That can be part of the route."

Rhodes didn't believe Rapper would come after the smaller still, but it was a possibility.

"Some fella named Schwartz called," Hack said. "He wanted you to know he's got that flyin' saucer gadget ready to take to Mr. Ellendorf. Said he'd get it to him tomorrow."

"Why not this afternoon?"

"He wanted that Benton fella to go with him. Said Benton could explain it better'n he could."

Rhodes wasn't sure what needed an explanation. Just turn it on and the saucers would stay away. It seemed simple enough, but maybe there was some secret to it.

"Some woman named Schafer called, too," Hack said. "The one that owns that antiques store in Obert. She wanted to talk to you about Jamey Hamilton. Something's been bothering her about him and his shop."

"That's all she said?"

"Yep. You want to call her or go to Obert?"

Rhodes remembered that Buddy was supposed to be checking on Hamilton. He asked Hack if Buddy had found anything new.

"Not that he mentioned. Didn't leave any report, either."

Rhodes thought he might as well make the short drive and see what Michal had to say. It might not be a bad idea to talk to Hamilton again while he was there. If Larry Crawford had been dealing with Jerry Kergan, Hamilton might know something about it.

"What about Benton?" Rhodes asked. "Any calls from him?"

"Not a word."

Rhodes would stop by Dooley's on the way to Obert. Benton and Muller might still be there, trying to find something on Kergan's computer. He would have thought they'd have found something by now, as eager as they'd seemed to get to work on the little project Rhodes had assigned them.

BENTON'S CAR was parked in the same place in the Dooley's lot where Rhodes had last seen it.

Rhodes glanced in the back window and noticed that the guitar case was missing. When he opened the restaurant door, he heard Benton's voice and the sound of the guitar. The math teacher was singing something to the tune of "The Ballad of Davy Crockett," but Rhodes distinctly heard the words "Sheriff Rhodes" in place of the name of the famous defender of the Alamo.

Benton stopped his picking and singing when Rhodes walked into Kergan's office. He was in Kergan's office chair, the guitar case lying on the floor beside him.

Mel Muller sat at the computer desk. She wasn't looking at the computer, however. She appeared much more interested in Benton than in Kergan's accounts.

"Hey, Sheriff," Benton said. "I didn't think you'd be back so soon."

Rhodes pointed out that soon was the wrong word. "I've been gone three hours," he said.

"Time flies when you're having a good time," Benton said, smiling at Mel.

"I guess it does," Rhodes said. He hadn't been having as much fun as Benton. "What's that song you were playing?"

Benton looked down at the guitar as if he hadn't known he was holding it.

"Just a little composition of my own," he said. "It's not quite finished. I was working on it, with a little help from Mel."

"I think I recognized the tune."

"You probably did. Sometimes I do parodies. You know, like Weird Al Yankovic."

Rhodes wasn't sure who Weird Al was, but he didn't ask. Benton was weird enough for him.

"I thought I heard my name mentioned."

"It's a tribute song," Benton said.

"A parody tribute song?"

"You could call it that. It's 'The Ballad of Sheriff Rhodes.' You want to hear it?"

"It's pretty good," Mel said. "Seepy's very clever at writing lyrics."

So it's *Seepy* already, Rhodes thought. Move over, Dr. Phil.

"I am good at lyrics," Benton said. "I write a lot of my own songs."

"I know," Rhodes said, "but I'm more interested in what you found out about Kergan's accounts."

"Oh," Benton said. "Nothing."

"Nothing at all?"

"Nothing you haven't seen already," Mel said. "We did a thorough search. There's nothing on that computer we haven't seen."

"He didn't use it much," Benton said. "He didn't download music, didn't have an eBay account, didn't even use his Web browser for anything more than checking the weather report now and then."

"And that's it?"

"That's it," Mel said.

Rhodes was disappointed. He'd hoped for something that would lead him to Rapper or Crawford, and all he had was a few figures that didn't really mean anything.

"Seepy and I are going to work together again," Mel said. "He's going to help me design your Web site."

"For free," Benton said. "Just another little part of my service to the community."

"How soon do you think you'll have it up and running?" Rhodes asked.

"It won't be long," Benton said. "Not with me helping."

"That's good news. Mikey Burns will be happy."

"Not that we care," Mel said.

Benton looked at her, but she didn't elaborate.

"You two had better leave now," Rhodes said. "I'll lock the place up."

"Are you sure you don't want to hear 'The Ballad of Sheriff Rhodes'?" Benton said.

"I'm sure," Rhodes told him.

First a book, and now a song, Rhodes thought. Before long, he was going to be the most famous person in Blacklin County.

Benton shrugged off Rhodes's refusal and turned to Mel. "It's almost time for dinner. We didn't take a break for lunch. Would you like to go to the Jolly Tamale?"

"I love Mexican food," she said.

Rhodes loved Mexican food, too, but having sneaked the Quarter Pounder at lunch, he knew he wouldn't be eating Mexican food for a while.

Benton put his guitar in its case, and he and Mel left. Rhodes looked around the office, saw nothing of interest, and went out, locking the door of the restaurant behind him.

TWENTY-EIGHT

MICHAL SCHAFER SAT IN an old ice-cream-parlor chair in front of her shop, fanning herself with an old cardboard fan printed on one side with an ad for a funeral home in Arkansas. Rhodes sat in the chair next to her. A small round-topped ice-cream-parlor table was between them. The chairs and table had been painted with white enamel.

After Rhodes admired the table and chairs, Michal told him about the activity at Jamey Hamilton's shop, which was closed at the moment. An old wooden awning that hung over all the stores along the block shaded them from the late-afternoon sun.

"Remember that I said something about how many customers he has?" Schafer said. "And how fast he got them out of there?"

Rhodes said that he remembered.

"I started thinking about that today. You might have noticed that I don't have a lot of customers myself, so I have time to think about things like that. Anyway, one reason he was so fast was that some of them looked just the same when they came out as they did when they went in."

"Which means?"

"Which means they didn't get haircuts, and if they didn't get haircuts, what did they get?"

Rhodes had an idea, the same one that Buddy had suggested, but before he could tell her what it was, she went on.

"I do have a few customers, and some people drop by just

to talk, so I've heard a few things about Mr. Hamilton today. About his cousin, mainly, and you know what I think?"

"You think Hamilton was selling bootleg whiskey out of his barbershop."

"You must be a mind reader, Sheriff."

"No. I was just thinking the same thing."

Hamilton's place was a small barbershop in an out-of-the way town, in a building located right on a highway. It was the perfect place to sell the whiskey. People from other counties could find it easily, and there was almost no risk involved in the buying and selling.

"I didn't know people still went in for that kind of thing," Michal said.

"Everything makes a comeback sooner or later," Rhodes said. "Otherwise, you antique dealers would be out of business."

"I'm about out of business anyway. You wouldn't want to buy this nice table and chair set, would you? I have two more chairs in the back of the store to make the set of four. I can give you a good price."

"I'll have to pass, but sooner or later someone will want them. Have you seen Hamilton today?"

"He hasn't been in. He's had a few customers come by looking for him."

"Did they stop or just drive on by?"

"A couple of them stopped. I asked if I could help them. They didn't say anything. They just left."

Rhodes got up and walked over to the barbershop. He looked in through the big plate-glass window, but all he could see was the empty shop, with its two barber chairs, its shelf of lotions and hair tonics, its big mirrors on both side walls. He wondered if anybody ever got an actual haircut there.

"Oh, yes," Michal said when he asked. "I've seen Jamey cutting hair every day. People seem to like his work."

Too bad he didn't stick with it, Rhodes thought, instead of taking up a sideline.

"I'm going to drive out to his house," Rhodes said, walking back over to the round table where Michal sat. "If he happens to come into the shop, it's all right if you mention that I'm looking for him."

"You don't think he'll flee the country?"

She meant it as a joke, but Rhodes was reminded of Rapper and Nellie, who had fled not only the country but the known universe.

"I hope he'll stick around," Rhodes said.

LARRY CRAWFORD'S rust-colored pickup sat under the chinaberry tree, where Rhodes had last seen it. The tree's leaves were already yellow, and the ground around it was littered with yellow berries.

This time, there was another pickup at Hamilton's house, a red Ford, parked next to Crawford's, so Rhodes figured both men were there.

Rhodes parked the county car, and when he stepped out, he heard people talking behind the house. He also smelled meat cooking on a grill.

He walked around the house and saw Crawford standing by a big black propane grill. The top of the grill was open and Crawford poked a long-handled fork into the steaks that sizzled above the low flames.

Hamilton sat in the shade of a pecan tree in a green plastic lawn chair, the kind that cost a couple of dollars at Wal-Mart. The tree was infested with webworms. The grayish webs were thick along most of the limbs. The worms, along with the drought, will kill the tree if Hamilton doesn't do something about them, Rhodes thought.

Hamilton didn't appear to be concerned with the webworms or with anything else. He held a glass of beer in one hand and a cigarette in the other. A low table beside him held another can of beer and an ashtray. A second chair stood on the other side of the table.

Hamilton saw Rhodes and raised the beer can in a kind of toast.

"Living the good life, I see," Rhodes said.

Crawford turned from the steaks. He wore a stained white apron that said LICENSED TO GRILL on the front in big black letters. He didn't look like a man lost in grief.

"Hey, Sheriff," he said. "Too bad we don't have enough for you, or I'd ask you to stay. Might be another beer in the fridge, though. How about it, Jamey?"

"Nope," Hamilton said, flicking ashes onto the dry grass beside the chair, not seeming to care if he caused a fire. "We just had the two."

Rhodes suspected he was lying, but he didn't care. His drink of choice was Dr Pepper.

"You come to tell me you caught the son of a bitch that killed my brother?" Crawford said. He turned the steaks over and closed the top of the grill. "Five more minutes and those'll be just right. Well, Sheriff? How about it?"

"I might know who did it," Rhodes said.

Crawford waved the fork. "You got a name? You tell me the name, and you won't have to worry about making an arrest. I'll take care of the son of a bitch for you."

Rhodes wanted to ask if Crawford planned to gut the killer with the meat fork, but he refrained.

"I can't tell you yet. What I want to talk about is that whiskey you and Terry were making."

Crawford grinned. "Now, come on, Sheriff, you know better than that. I already told you it was Terry who was making the whiskey. I'm the one tried to get him to stop,   remember? Even the land's in Terry's name. You ask my lawyer, and he'll tell you the same."

Rhodes was sure of that. He said, "Let's say I believe you. I guess if Terry was making the whiskey, Jamey wasn't cutting you in on any of the profits he made from selling it out of his barbershop."

Hamilton ground out his cigarette in the ashtray, set his beer can down on the table, and stood up.

"Are you accusing me, Sheriff?" he said.

"That wasn't an accusation. Just a statement. I have a witness."

Rhodes knew that nothing Michal had told him could be considered evidence. He'd just wanted to see how Hamilton would react.

"Probably that old bat that has the antiques next door to me," Hamilton said. "She never has liked me. Anyway, it's her word against mine. You won't find any whiskey in my shop. Maybe you've already looked. That'd be an illegal search, and I'll have my lawyer file on you in a New York minute."

Rhodes had often wondered why a New York minute was supposed to be any shorter than a Clearview minute, or a Philadelphia minute. Or any other minute at all, for that matter. He didn't think this was the time for a philosophical discussion of the topic, however.

"I haven't been in your shop. Michal Schafer will vouch for that."

Hamilton sat back down in the green chair. "It's a good thing you didn't go in. You gotta have a warrant for that. I know my rights."

According to the records, Hamilton had never been incarcerated, but he already sounded like a jailhouse lawyer to Rhodes, who was now convinced that Hamilton had been selling whiskey. Not much, maybe, but certainly enough to get him jailed if he'd been caught at it.

Crawford opened the grill and smoke rolled out.

"Looks like these steaks are ready. Time for you to be on

your way, Sheriff. Jamey and I'll be going inside to eat." He turned off the propane supply, and the flames in the grill died. "Like I said, we'd invite you to stay, but there's no more beer and just the two steaks."

He walked over to Rhodes and waved the two-pronged fork under his nose. A small piece of overcooked steak adhered to one prong.

"You hear what I'm saying, Sheriff? Don't make me have to stick a fork in you to prove you're done."

Rhodes was tired of listening to Crawford, and Hamilton, too, for that matter. And he didn't like being threatened. He grabbed the fork and jerked it out of Crawford's hand. The sudden movement made both his shoulder and chest twinge, but he didn't mind.

"You know what you need?" Rhodes said as Crawford stared at him openmouthed. "You need a chef hat. One with some kind of funny saying on it. Something like 'Kiss My Grits.' What do you think?"

"You took my fork," Crawford said.

Rhodes looked at the fork. "Sure enough. You weren't threatening me with it, were you? Because if you were, I'd have to arrest you."

Crawford started to say something, but Rhodes put up his empty hand to stop him.

"I know what you're going to say. You're going to say 'I'll call my lawyer.' But you can save your breath. I'm not going to arrest you. I'm not even going to keep your fork."

As he said that, he threw the fork at the dry ground, tines-first. The ground was so hard that the fork didn't penetrate it. It hit and bounced about six inches straight up before falling flat. Rhodes thought the hard ground might even have bent the tines. If that happened, Crawford would probably want to sue him.

Crawford picked up the fork and wiped it on the front of his apron. Hamilton sat where he was, not saying a word.

"You're the sheriff," Crawford said to Rhodes. "You can come here and throw my fork on the ground, and there's nothing I can do about it. Jamey, though, he owns this place, and he can ask you to leave. What about it, Jamey?"

"You want to leave, Sheriff?" Hamilton said. He didn't sound happy about having to say it. "I mean, if you're through causing trouble and all."

Rhodes was through. He'd found out what he wanted to know. Hamilton was guilty of selling whiskey, and Crawford was guilty of making it. They hadn't admitted it, and Rhodes might not be able to prove it about either of them, but he was convinced. It wasn't that their crime was so terrible, and it wasn't that they shouldn't pay for breaking the law. It was the fact that they felt like they were putting something over on him that bothered him most. He knew that wasn't a good thing, but he couldn't help it.

"I'll be leaving now," he said. "You two enjoy those steaks. They don't serve meals like that in the prison units. They don't have beer, either, and they don't allow smoking. You wouldn't like it there very much."

"Yeah," Crawford said. "That's why we're not going."

"You be careful on your way to town," Hamilton said. "And don't hurry back."

Rhodes left them there, both men laughing at their cleverness.

TWENTY-NINE

AFTER A HEARTY DINNER of vegetarian lasagna, Rhodes went out to play with the dogs in the backyard for a while. Even though it was well after dark, the heat hung on. Neither he nor the dogs could work up much enthusiasm, so after a couple of minutes, Rhodes made sure that Speedo's water dish was filled with clean water and then sat on the back steps.

While Yancey chased Speedo halfheartedly around the yard, Rhodes sat on the back steps and thought about the murder of Terry Crawford and the disappearance of Rapper and Nellie.

No matter how hard he tried, Rhodes couldn't make all the facts fit any scenario he could devise. It was like looking at a jigsaw puzzle with all the pieces laid out on the table but not finding any two that fit neatly together. Oh, you could jam one of the tabs into the place where it looked as if it belonged, but it was clear that it really didn't go there.

Why would Rapper kill Kergan? Rhodes had thought he knew the answer to that question, but it had turned out that he was wrong.

Why would Rapper kill Terry Crawford? That was something that needed considerably more thought. The most likely answer was that Terry was competition for Rapper, who had taken his usual direct route to getting rid of anyone who got in his way. If that was the case, however, Rapper certainly shouldn't have killed Kergan, who could have put him in touch with the people who'd been buying from the Crawfords.

A couple of other things were wrong, too, but Rhodes couldn't quite wrap his mind around them. He knew they were in there somewhere, slipping around just out of reach of his consciousness. He caught hints of them, but then they'd slip away from him.

He heard the telephone ring inside the house, but he didn't get up. If it was important, Ivy would come and get him. High in the sky, an airplane's light flashed in the darkness, moving from west to east. Rhodes wondered where the plane had been and where it was going. What were the people on it thinking about? Not about two murders in Blacklin County, he was sure.

Ivy came outside and sat beside him on the steps.

"That was Mikey Burns on the phone," she said. "What have you done to make him mad?"

"Nothing. I just got into the middle of an argument he was having with Mel Muller. I thought they liked each other, but I was wrong."

"About the department's Web site?"

"Yes. Is that what he called about?"

"That was one thing. He said he was holding you responsible for that Web site, and that if it wasn't on line by next week, you'd be sorry."

"Why would he say that to you?"

"Because I told him you weren't here and that I'd take a message."

"I am here, though."

Ivy patted his knee. "I thought you needed a break."

"You were right about that. Thanks. What was the other thing?"

"He said there'd been two murders in his precinct and that you hadn't done a thing about either one of them. He wants you to come in for a meeting tomorrow and make a report to him."

"I don't have to report to the commissioners."

"I think he knows that. He was just trying to throw his weight around a little."

"He should throw it at me, not you."

"I didn't mind," Ivy said. "He needed to let off some steam, and he did. I'm sure he feels much better now."

"I'd feel better if I had Rapper and Nellie in jail," Rhodes said.

"You'll catch them sooner or later."

"Right," Rhodes said.

WHEN RHODES WENT to bed that night, he thought that maybe everything would fall into place.

When he woke up the next morning, it hadn't happened. He was still as puzzled by everything as he'd been when he went to bed. His head didn't hurt, however, and the knot was smaller than it had been. The bruise on his chest was still colorful, but his shoulder was less sore. All in all, he had to believe things were getting better.

He went out to feed Speedo and check the water dish. It was another hot day, already in the eighties, and the sun was barely over the horizon. It's a dry heat, though, Rhodes told himself. That was supposed to be good. And so far, not a single person had asked if it was hot enough for him. That was good, too. It was only a matter of time until someone did ask, but he was glad of the temporary relief.

As he drove to the jail, something he'd thought of while sitting on the steps came back to mind, the idea that Rapper had killed Terry to get rid of the competition.

Rhodes believed that Rapper was fully capable of killing a man just to get rid of him, but the method didn't seem to be one Rapper would choose. A .25-caliber pistol? Rapper would prefer a .45, if not a twelve-gauge shotgun. Or a big Dodge pickup. Rhodes hadn't managed a good look at Nellie's pistol, but he was pretty sure it had been bigger than a .25. Nellie wasn't like Rapper, but he'd prefer a weapon with some stopping power.

That thought led him back to the Schwartzes. Max had told Rhodes he'd been wrong about Terry's having insulted Jackee. Had he just been trying to mislead Rhodes, or had he been telling the truth? Rhodes had believed him at the time, but that was when he'd thought Rapper was the killer.

There was no getting around the fact that Rapper had killed Kergan, however. Max couldn't be tied to that. Neither could Mikey Burns, though Rhodes wouldn't have minded pinning it on him. The black pickup, however, belonged to Rapper.

Rhodes arrived at the jail. He wondered what the bad news would be this morning. It didn't take him long to find out.

"Sonny Streeter's wife's left him again," Hack said before the door had closed behind Rhodes.

"We don't do divorce work," Rhodes said.

"Sonny don't want a divorce," Lawton said.

"What does he want, then?"

"He wants his keys back," Hack said. "Miz Streeter took 'em all with her. Took the car keys, house keys, and even the keys to his store."

Streeter owned a little video-rental store in a strip mall near the Wal-Mart. His wife, Sandy, worked there with him. They had frequent arguments about the operation of the store, the family finances, and other things. Sometimes the arguments got so loud that the other store owners would complain. Now and then, one of the Streeters would call to report the other for some petty thing. Though they never got violent, they separated every three or four months. They always got back together, and then things started all over again.

"Sonny says he's going to file on her for theft," Lawton said.

"I told him those keys were prob'ly community property," Hack said. "He doesn't own but half of 'em."

"We'll see what we can do about getting his half of them back," Rhodes said. "You tell Ruth to find Sandy and see if she can talk her into giving Sonny the keys."

"They'll be back together by tomorrow," Hack said. "They always are."

"We'll see," Rhodes said. "Is there any good news?"

"Could be. That Benton fella called. He was all excited, wants to talk to you."

Somehow, Benton hadn't struck Rhodes as being a morning person. He looked more like someone who preferred to sleep until around noon.

"When did he call?"

"'Bout a half hour ago. Here's his number."

Hack handed Rhodes a piece of notepaper with a telephone number scrawled on it in pencil. Hack didn't like pens.

Rhodes went to his desk and made the call. Benton answered on the first ring.

"You're up early," Rhodes said.

"I haven't been to bed, but that's not the point. I have a surprise for you."

"A good one, I hope."

"A good one. Write this down." Benton read off a Web site URL. "We were up most of the night getting it done."

"You and Mel?"

"That's right. She's great. She even knows math."

Yes, sir, Rhodes thought. Dr. Phil wouldn't stand a chance against me.

"I don't see how you got it done so fast."

"Mel had already started, so with my expertise and hers, we were able to do it all in one night. It was a long night, but we had fun putting it together. You're going to love it."

Rhodes hoped Mikey Burns loved it, but he wasn't going to tell Burns yet.

"Thanks," Rhodes said. "I know you did a great job, and I haven't even seen it."

"Yet another example of my helping out county law enforcement. Mel and I still have some tweaking to do, so don't worry if there are a few little problems. We'll take care of them. And don't bother to call me back after you've seen it. I'm going to bed."

Rhodes thanked him again and hung up. Then he read off the URL to Hack, who typed it into his computer.

"Would you look at that," Hack said.

The home page had a picture of the jail and a picture of Rhodes, along with contact information. There were other pages and other pictures, including one of Hack, who couldn't believe he was on the Internet.

"Where'd they get that?" he said. "I didn't know they had that."

Rhodes suspected that Mel had been in touch with Jennifer Loam, who'd taken some photos at the jail months ago.

"It's a good likeness," Lawton said. "Too bad they didn't get one of me to go on there. I guess they didn't dare. They didn't want all the women coming around, chattin' me up and interferin' with our business."

"That's bound to be it," Hack said. "Either that or they didn't want to scare anybody."

Lawton didn't respond to the gibe. Hack looked disappointed, but he soon turned back to the computer to look at the Web site.

"I didn't think they'd come up with anything this nice," he said after awhile.

Rhodes was pleased, too. He'd seen the Web sites of a couple of other departments, and he thought this one was as good as those and maybe even better. He didn't see any problems that needed tweaking. It's about time, he thought, that I got some good news.

The telephone rang, and Hack answered. He listened for a few seconds and then said to Rhodes, "It's for you. Max Schwartz."

Rhodes picked up his phone and said hello.

"I need you to go with me to see that Ellendorf guy," Schwartz said. "I just talked to Benton, and he told me to get off the phone and let him sleep."

"He's been busy all night. I thought you needed his help when you met Ellendorf."

"I wanted him to explain how the saucer repeller works. He made it sound complicated and logical."

"Ellendorf won't care about that, as long as it works. I guarantee it'll work. The less we have to tell him about it, the better."

"If you say so. I guess I could tell him how to turn it off and on, but I don't know where he lives."

"I'll pick you up and go with you. Where are you?"

"At my store."

"It's still early," Rhodes said. "I'll be there in an hour."

"I'll be waiting."

Rhodes spent the next hour working on his reports. He was just about caught up by the time he left to get Schwartz, who was waiting for him behind the counter. He was drinking coffee from a big green mug. No music was playing this time, and Rhodes missed it.

A small mahogany box sat on the counter in front of Schwartz. The box had two black knurled knobs on the front and three small red lightbulbs on top. The bulbs pulsed on and off in sequence. One lighted up, then two, then all three. After that, all went off. Then the first lighted up and went off. The second did the same, followed by the third, before the first sequence repeated. A distinct hum sounded as each bulb lighted on, and when all three were on at once, the hums made a pleasing chord.

"If that doesn't repel flying saucers," Rhodes said, "I don't know what will."

"So you like it?" Schwartz said.

"It's perfect. Are you ready to go?"

Schwartz took a swallow of coffee. "I'm ready."

THIRTY

ELLENDORF WAS THRILLED with the little machine Schwartz had made.

The box sat on his kitchen counter by the sink, the lights pulsing and humming. Ellendorf watched, fascinated.

"You control the lights with this knob," Schwartz said, touching the one on the left. "It turns the machine on and off."

"I don't want to turn it off," Ellendorf said. "I want it on all the time.

"It's all right to leave it on," Schwartz said, "but you'll need to change the batteries." He showed Ellendorf how to do that. "They'll last longer if you keep the volume low. That's what the other knob is for."

Ellendorf turned the volume up and down.

"I'll leave it set about in the middle, so I can hear it good. I really do appreciate this, Sheriff. You, too, Mr. Schwartz."

"Just call me Max."

"Max. You can call me Dave. How much do I owe you?"

"Not a thing," Rhodes said. "Mr. Schwartz is a graduate of the Citizens' Sheriff's Academy, and he made this because he's a public-spirited kind of a guy."

"That's right," Schwartz said. "I'm always glad to help out. If you ever need any musical instruments, repair work, or even a CD, you come by my store and I'll fix you up."

"I'll do that," Ellendorf said.

He shook hands with Schwartz and Rhodes and told them again how much he appreciated what they'd done.

On the way back to the store, Schwartz said, "Are you sure that thing will work?"

"All it takes is belief, and Ellendorf's more than ready to believe it. It'll work just fine. That's why I guaranteed it."

"What about those killings? Have you found out who did them?"

"I'm still working on that," Rhodes said. "Do you keep any kind of weapon at the store? For protection?"

"I'm not licensed to carry," Schwartz said, "and all I have under the counter at the store is a baseball bat. I'm not so sure it would help me if I came up against a robber with a gun, but Jackee doesn't like guns. So I don't have one. You don't still think I killed Crawford, do you?"

"No," Rhodes said. "I just like to be sure."

"You can check when you drop me off. I don't want you thinking I'm a killer."

"I don't need to check."

"I want you to. We'll both feel better about it."

"All right, then. I'll check."

THE BASEBALL BAT was a Louisville Slugger, solid black except for the brand and the player's signature in gold. It was an Alvin Dark model.

"Dark played for the New York Giants," Schwartz said as Rhodes hefted the bat. They called him 'Blackie.' I don't know if that's because he used black bats or not. He played so long ago that probably nobody even remembers him now."

"Where'd you get the bat?" Rhodes asked, putting it back under the counter.

"At a flea market. I like flea markets, but I don't get to go often now that I have the store."

"You should go to Michal Schafer's store in Obert. She has a lot of jun—antiques. Baseball cards, too. I don't know about bats."

"She probably doesn't need one. Nobody steals antiques."

Rhodes wasn't so sure about that. Judging from his experience, people would steal just about anything. Michal didn't seem like the type. On the other hand...

"I have to go," Rhodes told Schwartz. "I have some sheriffing to do."

SOMETHING HAD MADE all the pieces of the puzzle fly into place. Maybe it had been talking to Schwartz, or maybe it had been something else. Rhodes didn't care. He was now almost certain he had the whole picture.

Well, that wasn't true. Some of the pieces were still not in place, and he didn't have the *whole* picture, but he had most of it. It was a little fuzzy, and it wasn't the one he'd thought he'd see when the puzzle came together. That happens when you've lost the box and don't have a picture to guide you. And without a picture, you are likely to create one for yourself, one that doesn't really have as much to do with the puzzle as you think.

Rhodes's problem now was to prove that what he believed to be the true picture wasn't just another false image. He wasn't sure he could do that. He could put together a good circumstantial case, but he needed some hard evidence.

Or a confession. That would be nice, Rhodes thought, but he knew that Rapper wouldn't tell him anything even if Rapper could be found, which was looking less likely all the time.

Nellie might rat somebody out, if he could be separated from Rapper, but even that was doubtful. Besides, Nellie was going to be just as hard to find as Rapper.

The one piece of evidence that Rhodes had any hope of

finding was the pistol that had been used to kill Terry Crawford. He thought he might even have an idea now of where it might be, but he'd need a search warrant.

He didn't know what he'd do if the pistol wasn't where he thought it was. Search somewhere else, maybe, but by the time he did that, it would be too late. The pistol would be long gone.

It could be long gone already, for all Rhodes knew, but he didn't think so. There was no reason to get rid of it, since Rhodes was so far off the track.

He called Hack on the radio and told him to get in touch with Judge Parry, who'd make out the search warrant.

"You comin' by here before you pick it up?" Hack asked.

"Why?"

"Your friend Mikey Burns was by lookin' for you. He said if you came in, to keep you here till he got here. He wants to talk to you about something. He didn't look very happy. I think he's still mad about that car you wrecked."

"Rapper wrecked it, not me."

"Burns blames you, though. You oughta keep that in mind."

"Thanks for the warning. Did you tell him about the Web site?"

"No. I figgered you'd want to be the one to do that."

"You figured right. If he comes by or calls again, tell him I'm busy busting crimes."

"Like Sage Barton," Hack said.

"You've been reading the book."

"Yeah. Just a couple of pages now and then. I gotta tell you, old Sage Barton's one cool customer, bullets flyin' all around him, and he don't turn a hair."

"Just like me," Rhodes said. "You stop reading and call the judge."

"Yes, sir," Hack said. "Want me to send some backup?"

"Would Sage Barton need backup?"

"Sage Barton might be just like you, but you ain't just like Sage Barton, if you know what I mean."

"I know what you mean."

"So what about the backup?"

"Send some," Rhodes said.

THIRTY-ONE

RHODES HADN'T BEEN to a barbershop in a long time. In Clearview, most places that cut hair would take anybody who came in. Not the beauty shops, of course. Those were strictly female territory. But the old-fashioned men's barbershop was pretty much a thing of the past.

So Jamey Hamilton's place was a throwback to an earlier time. Even the mingled smells of hair tonic and aftershave reminded Rhodes of when he was a boy and the barber put a board across the arms of the barber chair for Rhodes to sit on so he'd be tall enough for the barber to reach.

"Need a little trim, Sheriff?" Hamilton asked when Rhodes came in.

A customer sat in the chair, a man Rhodes didn't recognize.

"I just want to talk," Rhodes said. "I'll sit and wait till you're finished."

"Fine by me."

Hamilton turned on the clipper he was holding, and it came to life with a hum that reminded Rhodes of the flying saucer repeller.

The interior of the shop was much cooler than it was outside, almost too cool. Rhodes picked up a newspaper and sat in a chair to wait. The newspaper turned out to be a copy of the *Clearview Herald* that was a week old. Rhodes put it on the chair next to him and watched Hamilton cut his customer's hair.

Hamilton was good with the clipper and scissors. When he was finished with the haircut, he combed the customer's hair.

Then he sharpened a straight razor on a leather strop hanging from the chair. After he was satisfied with the sharpness of the blade, he ran some water in a shaving cup and whipped up a lather with a short-handled brush. He applied the lather to the back of his customer's neck and shaved the neck smooth.

He washed off the razor, dried it, and put it back on a shelf. Then he applied lotion and talcum powder to the customer's neck. Finished now, he turned the chair around so the customer could have a look at himself.

"All right?" he asked.

The customer nodded.

Hamilton unpinned the protective cloth from around the man's neck and swept it off, shaking loose hair on the white tile floor. The man stood up, and Hamilton brushed him off with a whisk broom.

The man paid him and left without saying a word to Rhodes or Hamilton.

Hamilton stepped to the old-fashioned cash register sitting on the wide shelf in front of the mirror. Along with the register, the shelf held hair tonic and lotions. A narrower shelf underneath held the razor, the shaving cup, and the whisk broom.

The register was made of cast iron and was painted silver. It made a ringing sound when Hamilton punched in the sale, and the cash drawer popped out.

"Did you buy the cash register next door?" Rhodes asked.

Hamilton shook his head. "Came with the shop."

He put the money in the cash drawer and pushed it shut.

"It's an antique," Rhodes said. "Probably worth a good bit of money."

"I'll sell it if I start going broke." Hamilton got a broom and dustpan from a back corner of the shop. "I have to sweep up, and then I'll talk to you."

"Take your time," Rhodes said.

Hamilton swept the hair into the dustpan and took it into a back room. Rhodes heard him open a trash can and dump the hair into it. He seemed to stay in the room longer than was necessary, but eventually he came back into the shop.

"Where did you learn to cut hair?" Rhodes asked. "You do a nice job."

"My uncle taught me. He has a three-chair shop over in Nacogdoches."

"It's a useful skill," Rhodes said. "Might come in handy in prison."

Rhodes crossed his legs, resting his ankle on his knee, and leaned back in the chair.

"Prison? I don't know what you're talking about, Sheriff."

"It's where you'll be going. You and Larry."

Hamilton sighed. "Larry's told you over and over that Terry was the one making the whiskey, and I wasn't in on it with him. So why don't you give it up?"

"Because you and Larry killed Terry. I think Larry killed Jerry Kergan, too. You might even have been in on it."

"Look, Sheriff, I know somebody wrote a book about you, but that doesn't mean you should go making stuff up. Unless maybe you're gonna write a book yourself. Is that what it is?"

"I'm not writing anything except an arrest report."

"Well, you must be crazy, then."

"Maybe." Rhodes pointed to the cash register. "I guess a man who owns a barbershop takes in a good bit of money, even if he's not selling whiskey on the side. Is that right?"

"You can see I'm not exactly overrun with customers."

"Still, you have cash in there. A man needs to protect himself in case somebody wants to take his money. Isn't that right?"

Rhodes thought there would be more than a little cash in the register on a lot of days, not from haircuts, but from whiskey money. Nobody was going to give a check for moonshine.

Hamilton, looking a little nervous, moved over by the cash register.

"You're not fixing to rob me, are you?" he said.

"If I was thinking about it, what could you do to stop me?"

Hamilton's right hand twitched. "Nothing, I guess."

"Well, then, you won't mind if I take a look on that shelf, will you?"

Hamilton clenched his right hand into a fist. "You got no right to go looking on my shelf."

"I have a search warrant."

Rhodes pulled it from his shirt pocket with his left hand. He didn't offer to unfold it or hand it to Hamilton. Instead, he tossed it in Hamilton's direction.

Hamilton made no move to catch it. It dropped to the floor at his feet.

"I'm not picking that up," he said.

"It's your shop. You can do as you please."

"That's right. It's my shop, and you leaving is what would please me."

"Not until I make my search. I won't make a mess. I'm only going to look in one place."

"What if I do have a little protection? Anything wrong with that?"

"Not a thing. Unless the protection's a pistol that was used to kill somebody."

This was as far as Rhodes's figuring had led him. If the pistol was there, and he thought it was, Hamilton would either have to make a move or let Rhodes take a look at the shelf.

If the pistol wasn't there, well, Rhodes wouldn't be any worse off than he'd been before, or so he told himself.

Because of the other things on the shelf, he couldn't tell what else might be on it. Hamilton had not removed the other items all at the same time, and the pistol, if it was there, was most likely shoved back behind them, hidden by the overhang of the upper shelf.

"Well?" Rhodes said. "Are you going to let me take a look?"

"No," Hamilton said.

He reached onto the lower shelf, knocking the whisk broom to the floor, and pulled out a small automatic pistol. It was mostly hidden by his hand, but Rhodes thought it was a Browning, though it didn't really make much difference.

"Just stay right where you are," Hamilton said.

"You can't hurt me a whole lot with that thing," Rhodes said. "You couldn't even kill Terry with it. He got out of the trailer and bled to death while he was wandering around outside."

"Shut up," Hamilton said. "Come in here, Larry, and make him shut up."

Larry Crawford came out of the back room wearing a T-shirt that said REHAB IS FOR QUITTERS. Rhodes hadn't known he was there, though he'd guessed something had detained Hamilton when he was emptying the dustpan. It didn't seem fair that Hamilton had backup and Rhodes didn't. He wondered if Hack had forgotten to make the call to Ruth.

"You really oughta leave well enough alone, Sheriff," Larry said. "Things were going along just fine until you started nosing around."

"Blame Terry," Rhodes said. "He should have stayed inside."

"I thought he was dead. He was supposed to be blown up so I'd get the insurance money for the house and another bundle by suing the propane people. I'd have inherited the land, too."

"You could blame yourself a little bit," Rhodes said. "You should have bought some groceries at Wal-Mart or wherever you went that day. You shouldn't have taken your clothes out of the trailer, either."

Rhodes had noticed that there were no groceries in Crawford's pickup, but the importance of that fact hadn't registered with him at the time.

Also, there hadn't been any tracks in the field around the house, which meant that Rapper hadn't been there, not then.

And nobody could have found a new supply of unfunny T-shirts so soon.

"I figured I'd need the clothes, but not the groceries. Come on, Sheriff, we'll go out the back way."

"You planning to give me to Rapper?"

"That'd be a good idea. He doesn't like you much. But I can't do it. He's long gone. You messed that up real good. He and Jamey and I were planning a partnership. Would've been a sweet deal. Terry didn't like it, though, the little whiner."

That was what Rhodes had figured. Terry had been the one against the whiskey making, not Larry. Larry had just taken Terry's attitude and claimed it for his own.

"Rapper was going to move your still to get the evidence off the property. He should have done it sooner."

"Yeah, well, we didn't think you'd be looking in those woods. We like to have got you, though."

Rhodes had figured that part, too. Larry had been in the pickup with Rapper. He might even have been driving. Rhodes was sure now that Larry had killed Kergan or gotten Rapper to do it. Larry would have known when Kergan would go out to the back of the restaurant for a smoke, and he'd chosen that time to meet with him, maybe to introduce Rapper. When he'd seen Rhodes in the parking lot, either they'd panicked and killed Kergan by accident or they'd done it to keep Kergan from talking to Rhodes. Maybe they were afraid he'd already talked and therefore eliminated him as a witness before he could go on the record.

"Let's go," Hamilton said. He looked a little twitchy to Rhodes. "Somebody'll be coming in here any minute."

"You don't have that many customers now," Rhodes said, "not since you went out of the whiskey business."

"Shut up and stand up," Hamilton said, gesturing with the pistol.

Rhodes had been feeling a little uncomfortable anyway.

"All right," he said, but he didn't stand up.

His hand was already resting right over the ankle holster. He slipped it beneath his pants leg and pulled out the .38.

Hamilton's reactions were good, and he was shooting before Rhodes had the pistol up.

Luckily, Hamilton's aim wasn't as good as his reaction time. He missed Rhodes and shot the mirror behind him.

Seven years bad luck, Rhodes thought, throwing himself out of the chair as the glass shattered. He landed on his bad shoulder and yelled, not so much because it hurt but because he wished he'd jumped the other way.

He steadied himself amid the shards of the mirror and got off a couple of shots of his own, plinking a bottle of hair tonic and spattering it all over the cash register.

The sound of the shot echoed around the shop and off the tile floor. Hamilton's pistol had hardly made any noise at all.

Crawford scooted out through the back door without a word. Hamilton crouched behind the barber chair and fired at Rhodes again. The bullet smacked into the back of the chair Rhodes had been sitting in, but it didn't go through. The .25 really didn't pack much punch.

That didn't mean that Hamilton couldn't get lucky, however, and put one in Rhodes's eye. It wouldn't burst his skull, but it would kill him nevertheless. Rhodes wondered if this counted as a firefight and thought about what Sage Barton would do.

Probably he'd do some kind of mysterious martial arts move, flip over a couple of times, and land on the other side of the chair, after which he'd disarm Hamilton and cuff him.

Or maybe that's what Seepy Benton would do.

Not being either one of them, Rhodes had to resort to something within his capabilities, so he just shot Hamilton in the foot.

Hamilton screamed and dropped the little pistol. He squirmed on the floor, squealing and grabbing at his foot.

Rhodes stood up and went over to him. He toed the pistol and sent it sliding across the white tile, which was now spotted red by Hamilton's blood.

Gun smoke wafted all around them, and the sharp smell of it overwhelmed the shop's other odors.

Rhodes looked down at Hamilton. "If Crawford gets away, I'm going to come back and shoot you again."

"Crawford's not going anywhere," Ruth Grady said.

Rhodes's ears were ringing from the shots, and her voice sounded as if it were coming from the bottom of a well.

Rhodes turned and saw Crawford come back in, with Ruth behind him.

"I didn't think you were here," Rhodes said.

"I haven't been here long. I'm always too far away when Hack calls me. Anyway, I'm here now. I parked in the back just in case somebody tried to sneak out that way. Sure enough, somebody did."

"What if I'd been shot?" Rhodes said.

Ruth grinned. "I'd still have Crawford."

THIRTY-TWO

HAMILTON AND CRAWFORD were safely locked away, the TABC was coming for the stills, and Rhodes's head was fine. The bruise on his chest was still colorful, but his shoulder didn't hurt. With all that, he felt better about things in general.

Or course he could depend on Hack to change that.

"Mikey Burns still wants to talk to you about that car you wrecked," Hack said while Rhodes was working on his reports.

Rhodes took off his reading glasses and pressed the bridge of his nose between his thumb and forefinger.

"I didn't wreck the car."

"You know that, and I know that, but Mikey Burns is a different story. Besides, you ain't got Rapper and Nellie in a cell for him." Hack paused. "You'll get 'em sooner or later, though."

"Right," Rhodes said.

No matter what he said, however, he didn't think it was likely that Rapper and Nellie would be in a cell, either. They'd gone to ground wherever it was that they were hiding out, and they'd stay there until the next time they turned up in Blacklin County like a pair of bad pennies.

That reminded Rhodes of something, and he reached into his pocket. He pulled out the Indian Head penny he'd been carrying around and turned it over in his fingers. He didn't know if it had brought him any luck or not, but if he kept it in his pocket, he'd lose it sooner or later. He didn't want to do that, so he opened the middle drawer of the desk and dropped the penny in. It clinked against a pen.

"What's that?" Hack asked.

"Lucky penny."

"Wish I had one."

The telephone rang, and Hack answered. He talked for a while, then covered the receiver with his hand and turned to Rhodes.

"You might want to put that penny back in your pocket."

"Why?" Rhodes said.

"'Cause Mikey Burns says he and Judge Parry are in the judge's office and they want to talk to you."

"Tell them I'm on the way," Rhodes said.

THE JUDGE'S SECRETARY waved Rhodes into Parry's office without a word. Rhodes didn't know if that was a good sign or a bad one, but he didn't much care.

Parry sat behind his desk. He wore another of his expensive suits, as opposed to Burns, who had on another aloha shirt, this one with coconut trees, waves, and surfboards. Burns had a half smile on his face, as if he was looking forward to what was about to happen.

"Good afternoon," Rhodes said.

"Good afternoon, Sheriff," Parry said.

Burns just nodded.

"Take a chair, Sheriff," Parry said. "The commissioner has a few things he'd like to discuss."

Rhodes sat down and said, "I have a few things to discuss with you, too. First of all, the sheriff's department Web site's up and running. You might want to have a look at it when you get a chance." Parry had a computer on his desk, and Rhodes motioned to it. "In fact, now would be as good a time as any, if your computer's on."

"Why not?" Parry said, turning to the computer.

Rhodes told Parry the URL. The judge clicked on his Web browser and typed in the URL.

"That's a nice job, Sheriff," Parry said when the Web site came up. "I've been wondering when it would get done."

"I didn't do it," Rhodes said. "Melanie Muller did, along with a little help from one of the members of the Citizens' Sheriff's Academy. You know him, in fact. C. P. Benton."

"The math teacher?"

"That's right. 'The wild-eyed radical.'"

"How much did he charge?"

"Nothing at all. He donated his time because he's a public-spirited citizen."

Burns got up and walked over to look at the computer monitor. Parry continued to click on the Web site pages, but Burns made no comment on them. Rhodes wasn't surprised. Since there was nothing he could criticize, Burns wouldn't say anything at all.

"Benton's also helping out with some other things," Rhodes told Parry.

"Not legal or criminal matters, I hope," the judge said.

"No, just looking out for some people who otherwise might not be able to get help. Hallie Owens, for one."

"What kind of troubles does she have?"

"Imaginary animals," Rhodes said. When Parry looked puzzled, Rhodes added, "She's lonesome. Calls the department about animals in her house even when there aren't any."

"We don't need that kind of thing," Burns said, looking up from the monitor. "You should be solving real crimes, not looking for animals that don't exist."

"Benton's solved the animal problem," Rhodes said. "At least for now."

"Maybe he's not as bad as I thought," Parry said.

"He's a little strange," Rhodes said, "but he's all right."

"I'll bet he still causes trouble about the appraisal caps."

"I couldn't say about that," Rhodes said.

"The Web site is all right," Burns said, getting back to the primary topic. "It looks like I hired the right person to work on it."

Rhodes had known Burns would take the credit, but that was fine. Burns had hired Muller, after all, and the fact that she'd have finished long ago if he hadn't treated her shabbily didn't need to be mentioned.

"What worries me is the murders we've had," Burns said. "I don't like to think we have a killer running around loose. What have you done about that, Sheriff?"

"I've made an arrest," Rhodes said. "Larry Crawford and Jamey Hamilton are both locked up in the jail right now."

"What?" Burns said. "Crawford killed his own brother? Are you sure?"

Rhodes didn't want to say anything that might prejudice the judge.

"Let's just say that they're alleged to have committed certain crimes."

"How did you catch them?"

"Good police work," Rhodes said.

Burns went back to his chair. He didn't look nearly as pleased as he had when Rhodes had come in.

"Do they have a lawyer?" he asked.

"I don't know," Rhodes said. "Crawford hired Randy Lawless to work on his wrongful death suit, which I don't think will fly now. Maybe Lawless will stick with him."

"Maybe," Burns said, looking a little happier.

Rhodes didn't really think Lawless would stick. There wouldn't be any payoff, and Crawford couldn't afford Lawless's fees. It would be ironic if Lawless was chosen as Crawford's court-appointed attorney, but that wasn't anything that would be proper to discuss.

"Did you get any help from your academy students on the case?" Parry asked.

"Only in the usual way of things," Rhodes told him, not seeing the need to mention he'd asked Benton to look at Kergan's computer. "Benton lives out near the Crawfords' place, and he might be a witness."

Rhodes thought it was time to change the subject, so he said, "Max Schwartz has been helping out, too. He built a flying saucer repeller for Dave Ellendorf."

Parry laughed. Even Burns had to smile. Everybody knew about Ellendorf's problems with the flying saucers.

"So what you're telling me is that there aren't any vigilantes on the loose in Blacklin County," Parry said, "and the academy was a good idea after all."

Rhodes smiled. "It might have been," he said.